Hunting For
A Job

馬上搶救職場的英文面試！

求職面試

MP3

必備 英文

張瑜凌 編著

國家圖書館出版品預行編目資料

求職面試必備英文 / 張瑜凌編著
-- 二版 -- 新北市：雅典文化，民107. 01
面；　公分. -- (全民學英文；46)
ISBN 978-986-5753-96-2(平裝附光碟片)

1. 英語　2. 面試　3. 讀本

805. 18　　　　　　　　　106021396

全民學英文系列　46

求職面試必備英文

編著／張瑜凌

美術編輯／王國卿

封面設計／姚恩涵

法律顧問：方圓法律事務所／涂成樞律師

總經銷：永續圖書有限公司　　CVS代理／美璟文化有限公司
永續圖書線上購物網　　　　　TEL：(02) 2723-9968
www.foreverbooks.com.tw　　FAX：(02) 2723-9668

出版日／2018年01月

雅典文化

出版社　22103　新北市汐止區大同路三段194號9樓之1
　　　　　TEL　(02) 8647-3663
　　　　　FAX　(02) 8647-3660

【前　言】

英文面試真簡單！

當你在職場上打滾多年後，想要更進一步挑戰更具有挑戰性的工作時，「換工作」是選項之一；當你面對全球地球村零距離、零時差的分秒必爭的職場競爭時，「找一個能發揮所長的工作」是選項之一。

當你有機會到外商公司上班時，除了書面履歷的資格審查之外，「英語面試」是您與面試官面對面的第一次接觸。

根據一份人力資源調查的報告顯示，大部分的面試官在應徵剛開始的十分鐘之內，就已經決定此人是否適任此工作；沒有人能在短短的一次面試過程中，就對一個人百分之百的瞭解，因此幾分鐘之內的印象就會左右面試官的決定，這就是「第一印象」所發揮的功效。

如何在短短的幾分鐘之內，用英文完整地自我行銷？你有幾個重點需要掌握：

一、 自我介紹

二、 學經歷介紹

三、 對工作期望

四、 自我的生涯規劃

　　本書特別針對以上各點，做例句的說明，讓您在最短的時間內，有效率地、分門別類地學好用「英文面試」的技巧。

　　除此之外，本書還附有學習光碟，讓您仔細聆聽，邊看邊聽邊跟著念，只要每日重複練習，就能事半功倍，加強你學習用英文表達自己的能力。

【學習說明】

工欲善其事，必先利其器！

　　一份正確的學習教材，更能幫助您在學習英文的路途上，進步神速、突飛猛進！本書根據各種求職的情境，彙整編撰相關的英文例句，讓您在求職路上更為順利！

一、實用例句

> ✠ We have received your resume, and we would like to ask you to come here for an interview.
> 我們已經收到你的簡歷，我們想約你來此面試。

　　本章節共有 17 個單元，每一個單元都有相關的類似用法，您可以根據實際的需求，針對自己比較不熟悉的議題多加練習。

二、 實用會話

Unit 1 電話通知面試

Ⓐ : May I speak to Miss Jones?
　　我要找瓊斯小姐。

Ⓑ : Speaking.
　　我就是。

　　本章節共有 34 個單元，利用情境式對話方式，模擬實際可能發生的會話，讓您更加瞭解面對面試官時，您該有的臨場反應。

三、 人事廣告

人 事 招 聘 ◦◦◦ 客 服 部 主 管

⊙**Customer Service Sup.**

Management exp., customer service oriented

Fluency in English both speaking and writing

University degree

⊙**客服部主管**

有管理經驗，以為顧客服務為導向

英文說寫流利

大學畢業

　　當您想要尋找新工作時，「人事廣告」是您第一個探詢的目標，看得懂人事廣告，也才能找到最適合的工作。本章節歸類出多種的職務招聘廣告，您可以針對應徵的職務及相關的公司簡介、職務說明等，多方練習閱讀及理解能力。

四、 履歷及自傳

【 Resume Sample 】 Education

Maria Jones

Address:	No. 40, Lane 90, Sec. 2, Jhongshan Rd., Banciao Dist, New Taipei City. 220, Taiwan (R. O. C.)
Phone:	(02) 8467-3663
E-mail:	yadan@tpts5.seed.net.tw
Objective:	To obtain a position in financial analyst
Certificate:	CPA
Education:	B.S. in Economics to be obtained in June 2002

Related courses and scores on the 100 marking system:

Investment	86
Macroeconomics	90
Economic Decision-making	80
Accounting Principles	92
Money and Banking	84
Financial Management	92
Finance and Tax	92
Cost Accounting	85
Management Accounting	90
Economic Law	82

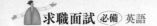

　　當您有看中意的工作時，您就必須有一份完整的履歷及自傳，不但能幫您在面試主管面前增加加分印象，也有助您在眾多應徵者中脫穎而出。

【前　言】英文面試真簡單！

目錄

Part 1 實用例句

Part 2 實用會話

Part 3 人事廣告

Part 4 履歷表及自傳

Part

1

實用例句

當你面試所使用的語言為中文時，一般人都能對答如流，但是當你面對外籍主管面試時，許多人往往會亂了手腳，認為自己的英語不夠流暢，其實這是你的心理作用，就好比你面對一個講中文不甚流暢的外國人時，一般人多會用鼓舞、讚美的態度鼓勵對方，同理，只要能掌握基本的英語溝通、表達能力，你對英語的用心表達，雇主通常會用比較寬容的心態接受。

英文面試最重要的應對技巧就是「自信心」，因為英語不是你的母語，所以你的遣詞用字必須簡單而明瞭，最忌諱的是用一些艱澀的語法作自我介紹。

以下單元特別針對面試時，可能使用到的英文語句，分門別類整理，先提供雇主可能提出的問句，再對應出你可以回答的答案，您可以依照自己的狀況擇一背誦。

Man proposes, God disposes.
謀事在人，成事在天。

Unit 1 面試開場白

Question
·面試官提問·

001 We have received your letter.
I would like to talk with you regarding your qualifications for this position.
我們已收到你的信。
我想和你談談關於此職位應徵的事。

002 We have received your resume, and we would like to ask you to come here for an interview.
我們已經收到你的簡歷,我們想約你來此面試。

003 Would you like to say something briefly about yourself?
請你簡單地自我介紹一下好嗎?

004 Tell me about yourself.
說一下你的情況。

005 Would you tell me about yourself?
Something like where did you go to school?
可以介紹一下你自己嗎?
像是你在哪一所學校讀書?

006 What kind of contribution do you feel you could make to our company and how long would it take?
您覺得自己能爲本公司做些什麼貢獻？需要多長時間？

007 You can describe yourself.
你可以形容一下你自己。

008 Let's talk about your college work and your experience.
我們聊一聊您的大學學習和工作經歷。

009 What kind of person do you think you are?
您覺得自己是怎樣的一種人？

010 What job are you applying for?
你想做什麼樣的工作？

011 What kinds of problems do you handle the best?
你最擅長處理什麼問題？

012 What is your greatest achievement?
你最大的成就是什麼？

013 I need your resume, please.
我需要你的履歷。

014 Do you have a resume with you?
你帶履歷表了嗎？

015 Do you bring your resume and your certificates with you?
你把簡歷和證書都帶來了嗎？

016 I have expected you for this whole week, Mr. Jackson.
傑生先生，我已經期盼你的到來一整個星期了。

017 Nice to see you.
很高興認識你。

Answer
・應徵者回答・

018 My name is Chris. I am thirty-five years old.
我名叫克里斯，今年35歲。

019 I'm here for the advertised job last Monday.
我來應聘上週一廣告的職位。

020 I would like to apply for the secretary.
我想申請秘書一職。

021 I would like to apply for the administrative assistant reporting to the managing director.
我想申請總經理助理一職。

022 I know you have an opening for an editor.
我知道貴公司編輯職位有空缺。

023 I saw your ad in CNS Times.
我在《CNS時報》上看到了貴公司刊登的廣告。

024 I learned from the classified ad in Monday's newspaper that you are looking for an English teacher.
我從星期一報上的分類廣告中知道，你們要找英文老師。

025 I look forward to talking further with you about the advertised position.
我希望能和您就廣告的職位進一步談談。

026 I learned about it from your advertisement in the newspaper.
我是從報紙上你的廣告獲知的。

027 I would like to change my present job because of the transportation problem.
因爲交通問題，我想改變我目前的工作。

028 I come at your invitation for an interview.
我是應你之邀來參加面試。

29 I come at your invitation for an interview.
It's nice to meet you, Mr. Anderson.
我是應你之邀來參加面試。
真高興見到你，安德森先生。

30 I am very happy that I am qualified for this
interview.
能獲得這個面談機會我非常高興。

031 My name is Sophia.
I think I am qualified for the job.
我的名字叫蘇菲亞。
我想我能勝任這項工作。

032 I worked in CNS Company before I applied for
this job.
應徵此工作前，我是在CNS公司上班。

033 Your company will benefit from gaining a
young energetic, bright person.
貴公司能透過雇用一個充滿活力、聰明的年輕人
而獲益。

034 I look forward to discussing with you in ways
which I could contribute to BCQ's continued
growth.
我希望能跟您談談，讓您知道我在哪些方面能為
BCQ公司的持續發展做出貢獻。

035 I'd welcome the opportunity to meet with you in person to explain my credentials more fully.
我希望能親自和您見面,更加詳細地談談我的任職條件。

036 Nice to see you, sir.
很高興認識你。

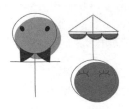

Unit 2 應徵原因

1 實用例句
2 實用會話
3 人事廣告
4 履歷表及自傳

Question
·面試官提問·

37 I see by your application that you worked at IBM for two summers.
What kind of work did you do?
我看見你的申請書中說你有兩個暑假是在IBM公司打工。
您做的是什麼工作？

038 Who referred you to this company?
誰介紹你來這家公司的？

039 Why should I hire you?
我為什麼要錄用你？

040 Why do you choose the job we offer?
你為什麼選擇我們提供的這份工作？

041 Why do you apply for this job?
你為什麼申請這份工作？

042 What made you decide to join TEXAS INSTRUMENTS?
你為什麼要加入德州儀器公司？

043 Why do you come here for a job?
你為何到此地來找工作？

044 Why did you choose to come here for a job?
你為何選定到此地來謀職？

045 Do you think you are qualified for this work?
你認為你能勝任這份工作嗎？

046 What makes you think you're qualified to work for us?
您為什麼覺得自己能勝任本公司的工作？

047 Are you able to take this job?
你能擔任這種工作嗎？

048 I'm interviewing 30 people for this job.
Tell me why I should hire you?
這個工作我面試了 30 位求職者。
告訴我，我為什麼要聘用你呢？

049 Why are you applying to Intel Company?
您為什麼要向英特爾公司求職？

050 Why do you want to work for us?
您為什麼想在本公司工作？

051 Why do you want to apply for a job at Wal-Mart?
你為什麼要到威瑪來申請工作？

052 How come you want to work here?
你為何要到這兒工作呢？

053 Why did you apply to our organization and what do you know about TSMC?
你為什麼申請本公司的職位，你對台積電的情況了解多少？

054 Why are you interested in this job, and what are your expectations?
您為什麼對這份工作感興趣？您對這份工作有什麼期望？

055 Why are you interested in working for our company?
為什麼有興趣在我們公司工作？

056 What is your ideal job?
您理想的工作是什麼？

057 May I know what has made you decide to apply for a position as secretary here?
我能知道你為什麼來此申請秘書一職嗎？

058 What made you choose this job?
你爲什麼選擇這個工作？

059 Thank you for your interest in this position.
Why do you consider yourself qualified for the job?
謝謝你對本公司這個職務感興趣。
爲何你認爲自己有符合這職位的資格？

060 What interest do you have most about this job?
你對這份工作最感興趣的是什麼？

061 Why are you interested in this job?
你爲什麼對這份工作這麼感興趣？

062 Why are you interested in working with this company?
你爲什麼對在本公司工作感興趣？

063 Why do you feel you will be successful in this work?
你爲什麼覺得你能勝任這份工作？

064 Why did you take up a job in the banks?
你爲什麼選擇銀行業這一種工作？

065 Why do you wish to work here?
你爲什麼要來此工作？

066 Do you think you are over-qualified?
你認為你資歷過高嗎？

067 Do you prefer part-time or full-time work?
你喜歡兼職還是全職？

Answer
•應徵者回答•

068 I think my qualifications and experience
perfectly match what you are looking for.
我認為我具備的資格及經驗完全符合你們的需
求。

069 I want this job because I know I can do a good
job.
我想要這份工作，因為我知道我能做得很好。

070 I think that my technical background is helpful
for you.
我覺得我的技術背景對你們有幫助。

071 I have enough knowledge to market the
products of your company.
我有足夠的知識來推廣貴公司的產品。

072 With my education, experience and perseverance, I'm sure I can perform my duties quite well.
我有這樣的學歷、經歷和毅力，我相信自己一定能好好表現。

073 I believe my record and experience can establish my competency to perform the work for which I am applying.
我相信我的學歷和經歷可以證明，我能勝任所申請的職位。

074 Because I know my unique training would be an asset to you, I am eager to become a member of your staff.
我知道我所受的特別培訓對貴公司會很有用，所以我渴望能成為你們的一員。

075 My training, education and personal qualities justify my application for the position.
我所接受的培訓、教育及所具備的人格特質，使我符合該職位的要求，特提出申請。

076 My education and experience is a match with the qualities you're looking for.
我的學歷和經歷正符合你們的要求。

077 My technical background is helpful.
我的技術背景很有幫助。

078 My educational background and professional experience make me qualified for the job.
我的教育背景和專業經驗使我能夠勝任這項工作。

079 Can Amazon use a hardworking employee like me who wants to learn and contribute to the success of the company?
亞馬遜公司是否能聘用我這種人？我勤勞好學，願為公司的發展效力。

080 If you think I can be an asset to this company and hire me, I will develop my potential better while at the same time making my contribution to this company.
如果您認為我對貴公司有用，聘用了我的話，我會更加努力地開發潛能，為公司作貢獻的。

081 The position would offer me exactly the kind of challenge and opportunity that I have hoped my master's degree would bring.
該職位正好提供了我希望的碩士學位能夠帶來的挑戰和機遇。

082 Your company is the largest and best one in this line of business.
貴公司在這一行裡，是最大最好的公司。

083 Because the working conditions and surroundings are excellent-all conducive to the further development of my abilities.
貴公司的工作情形和環境那麼好，而且對我未來技能的發展又有絕大的好處。

084 Because Dell has a good sales record.
因為戴爾(公司)有良好的銷售記錄。

085 Because I can learn new things in your company, at the same time I can offer my services to you.
因為我可以在貴公司學到新的東西，同時能為你們提供服務。

086 Because your operations are global, so I feel I can gain the most from working in this kind of environment.
因為你們公司的運作是全球化的，我覺得可以在這樣一個環境中工作會有最大的收穫。

087
"Good command of computer knowledge; sound intercultural communication skills" describes the person you want, and I believe I am that person.

你們所需要的是具有「豐富的電腦知識、突出的跨文化交流技能」的人,我相信自己就是這種人。

088 By referring to the enclosed resume and contacting the people I list as references, you will be able to acquire an overall picture of my specialized qualifications.

您可以從我附上的簡歷和其中列出的推薦(介紹)人那裡,全面了解我的專業才能。

求-職-面-試 小建議

　　在你準備要參加面試前,一定要對所面試的企業進行瞭解,例如公司的特性、企業的文化或是你所應徵職位,因為主管通常喜歡問應徵者之所以對此工作有興趣的原因。當你對這份工作或企業有一定程度的瞭解時,自然會對此問題不會陌生,你頭頭是道的回答也會為你的面試加分,容易在眾多應徵者中脫穎而出。

Unit 3 學歷背景

Question
·面試官提問·

089 Have you graduated from college?
你大學畢業了嗎？

090 Tell me about your educational backgrounds.
說一下你的教育背景。

091 Would you tell me what educational background you have?
請你告訴我有關你的教育背景好嗎？

092 What kind of education have you got?
你受教育的情況如何？

093 Which school or university did you attend?
你上那所學校或大學？

094 Where did you go to school?
你在哪一所學校讀書？

095 Which school of college did you attend?
你曾就讀於哪所學院？

096 What university do you attend?
你就讀於哪所大學？

097 What university are you attending?
你就讀哪所大學？

098 Which university did you graduate from?
你畢業於哪所大學？

099 Where did you receive your master degree?
你在哪裡獲得碩士學位的？

100 What university did you graduate from?
你從哪所大學畢業的？

101 When and what university did you graduate from?
你何時從哪所大學畢業？

102 What did you learn?
你學的是什麼？

103 Which school or college did you attend?
你曾經上過那間學校或大學？

104 What's your degree in?
你拿的是什麼專業的學位？

105 What did you major in college?
你在大學讀那一系？

106 What did you take up in college?
你大學讀什麼？

107 What was your major?
你主修什麼？

108 What was your major at college?
你在大學主修什麼？

109 What subject did you major in university?
你在大學主修的科目是什麼？

110 What were your major and minor subjects?
你主修和副修什麼科目？

111 What was your speciality?
你學的是什麼專業？

112 What was your major and why?
你的專業是什麼？為什麼要選這個專業？

113 What did you specialize in?
你學的是什麼專業？

114 Why did you take your particular program of studies?
你為什麼要選擇這個專業？

115 Why did you take Journalism as your major?
你為什麼選新聞業？

116 What made you decide to study English?
你為什麼會決定讀英語的呢？

117 What determined your selection of Business Administration as your field of study?
你為什麼決定要學企業管理呢？

118 Why did you take Business Administration as your major?
你為什麼學企業管理？

119 What courses did you enjoy the most? The least? Why?
你最喜歡什麼課程？最不喜歡什麼課程？為什麼？

120 What courses did you like the most?
你最喜歡那幾個科目？

121 Which courses did you like the best?
哪些課程你最喜歡？

122 What was your graduation thesis on?
你畢業論文是什麼題目？

123 What is the extent of your formal education?
你的最高學歷是什麼？

124 What degrees and diploma have you earned?
你取得了什麼學位和文憑？

125 Have you studied any courses related to the post you are applying for?
你曾修讀與你申請的這份工作相關的科目嗎？

126 What do you think the relationship is between the subjects you have taken and the job you are seeking?
你認為你曾修讀的科目和你申請的這份工作有何關係？

127 What made you decide to study Economics?
你為什麼決定修讀經濟學？

128 How are your grades in Taiwan University?
你讀台灣大學成績如何？

129 What scores did you get at school?
你在校時成績如何？

130 How were your scores in university?
你大學時的成績如何？

131 In what subject did you get the highest marks?
你哪個科目得分最高？

132 What was your best subject in college?
大學時你哪個科目成績最好？

133 How are you getting on with your studies?
你功課情況如何？

134 What's your best subject?
你最好的科目是什麼？

135 What was your favorite subject at school?
在校時你最喜歡的科目是什麼？

136 Which subject were you best interested in?
你對哪一科最有興趣？

137 What subjects did you concentrate on while attending university?
大學期間，你把注意力主要放在哪些課程的學習上？

138 How is your score in English?
你的英語成績是多少？

Answer
・應徵者回答・

139 Now I am a graduate student at the same university studying International Trade.
現在我仍然在同一所大學的國際貿易系讀研究院。

140 I am still a student.
我還是學生。

141 I graduated from Taiwan University.
我從台灣大學畢業的。

142 I've graduated from college.
我已經大學畢業了。

143 I graduated from school in 2003.
我是在2003年畢業的。

144 I graduated from Michigan State University in June, 2003.
我2003年6月畢業於密西根州立大學。

145 I am a postgraduate at Taiwan University.
我在台灣大學讀研究院。

146 I have a Bachelor of Arts degree.
我有個藝術學士學位。

I majored in Business English.
我主修的是商業英文。

In college, my major was International Management.
在大學的時候我主修的是國際管理。

I got a degree in journalist.
我有新聞傳播學士學位。

I've got a MBA in business studies.
我獲得了企管學士學位。

I received two master's degrees.
One is master of Telecommunication Engineering from Taiwan University, and the other is MBA from Washington University.
我獲得了兩個碩士學位。
一個是台灣大學的通訊工程碩士學位，另一個是華盛頓大學的企管碩士學位。

The MBA degree I will receive in June from Florida University has given me a broad foundation of business knowledge.
我具有廣博的商務知識，並將於今年6月獲得佛羅里達大學的企管碩士學位。

153 I am a graduate of Taiwan University of
Science and Engineering.
我是台大理工學院畢業生。

154 I am a college graduate.
我是大學畢業生。

155 I have a B.S. degree.
我獲有理學士學位。

156 I am a graduate student at Chinese University.
我是中文大學研究生。

157 I did my thesis on "Self-knowledge of
Journalism".
我做的論文題目是「新聞從業的自覺」。

158 I majored in Liberal Arts.
我主修人文科學。

159 English teaching was my major.
我主修英文教學。

160 I majored in Economic and Trade English.
我主修的是商用英文。

161 I liked international trade and international relations the best.
我最喜歡國際貿易和國際關係。

162 My favorite subject was history.
我最喜愛的一科是歷史。

163 Because I was interested in journalism and I wanted to become a reporter.
因為我對新聞有興趣，我想要做一名記者。

164 Because it is an fast-changing profession.
因為它是一門千變萬化的行業。

165 I took business administration as my major because there are greater demands for a man with these qualifications.
我學企業管理是因為這種人才很吃香。

166 They are above average 90.
I have worked hard at my major subject.
我的平均成績在90分以上。
我對主修科目特別用功。

167 I have consistently achieved high marks in mathematics.
我的數學成績一直很好。

168 I majored in Industrial Engineering and minored in Management, and I took eighty hours computer courses.

我的主修專業是工業工程，輔修專業是管理，還修了80小時的電腦課程。

169 I am presently a junior accounting major at Taiwan University.

During the past years, I have taken courses in accounting, taxation, finance, investments, auditing, and business law.

我是台灣大學會計專業三年級學生。

過去這段時間，學習了會計、稅收、財務、投資、審計和經濟法等課程。

170 As administration is an important aspect of any field, I knew it would aid me in any profession.

行政管理在我的領域佔著重要地位，我認為無論做那一行它都會對我有用的。

171 Because I wanted to work for the government in the administration offices.

因為我想在政府的行政機構工作。

172 My major at the university is just in line with the business scopes your company deals in.
我大學所學專業與貴公司的業務範圍相吻合。

173 I have developed excellent organizational skills by working on two major projects.
我曾參與兩個重大計畫，培養了出色的組織才能。

174 You will find that my college training provides an excellent foundation for the position for which I am applying.
我的大學教育，為我應聘的職位打下了堅實的基礎。

Unit 4 認證 / 推薦

175 Have you got any diplomas?
你有什麼證書嗎？

176 What qualifications have you got?
你有什麼資格證書嗎？

177 What qualifications do you have with you?
你有帶什麼資歷證明？

178 What certificates of technical qualifications have you obtained?
你有何種技術資格證書？

179 Let me see your references.
讓我看一下你的推薦信。

180 What additional training and schooling have you had?
您還上過其他的什麼學校或受過其他的什麼訓練？

181 Do you have a portfolio of your previous work?
你有沒有以前的作品集？

82 Can you furnish a letter of recommendation from IBM?
能請IBM公司提供你一份推薦書嗎？

83 How can you prove yourself?
你如何證明你自己呢？

84 Have you had any training in computer networks?
你參加過電腦網絡方面的培訓嗎？

85 Would your present and former employers give you recommendations?
你現在和以前的老闆都會給你寫推薦函嗎？

Answer
•應徵者回答•

186 Here is my certificate of merit.
這是我的獲獎證書。

187 I have a certificate of Spoken English Test.
我有英語口語證書。

188 I got a teacher's certificate two years ago.
我兩年前取得教師資格證書。

189 I am a certificated English teacher.
我是持有資格證書的英文老師。

190 I've got an Associate Professor's Qualification Certificate.

我獲得了副教授資格證書。

191 I have eight years' accounting experience and just received my CPA designation.

我有八年會計工作經驗，並且剛剛獲得註冊會計師認證。

192 I elected 6 computer courses and attended a 100-hour English training course.

我選修了 6 門電腦課程，參加了 100 小時的英語培訓。

193 I took a two-year training course for managers.

我參加過二年的管理培訓課程。

194 I have studied six months in a on-the-job marketing training program with satisfactory results.

我參加過為期六個月的行銷學在職培訓，成績合格。

195 I took all the courses useful for computer programming.

我學過所有對電腦程式有用的課程。

96 I have been well trained for that kind of work.
我接受過從事那項工作的良好訓練。

97 I was trained for that kind of job.
我受過這類工作的培訓。

98 My training and experience suit the job well.
我的經驗和所受的訓練使我很適合做這份工作。

99 I am a highly trained and practiced system analyst.
我是一位受過嚴格培訓、經驗豐富的系統分析員。

200 I have received the secretarial training for six months.
我曾接受過六個月秘書訓練。

201 I have participated in a secretary-training program.
我參加過秘書培訓班,學完了所有的課程。

202 I have just graduated from Taiwan University, but I served two terms of internship with the IT industry in the past year.
我剛從台灣大學畢業,但在去年我在IT產業實習了兩個學期。

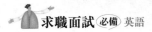

203 n addition to studying the prescribed courses in business administration, I selected electives such as computer and English courses to help me in my career objective.

我不但修了工商企業管理方面的規定課程，而且還選修了電腦和英語等課程，對我的工作能力有很大的提高。

204 My performance at the internship was so impressive that the manager wrote a letter of appreciation to my department.

我在實習時的表現很突出，經理還為此給我們科系寫了封感謝信。

205 I have never worked before. I just finished school. Would it be alright if the recommendations were from friends of the family?

我從來沒有做過事情，我剛剛離開學校。假如我從家裏的朋友那一方面要來推薦信可以嗎？

Unit 5 工作能力

Question
·面試官提問·

06 What do you think about your qualifications?
你認為你能勝任工作嗎？

07 Have you any experience with a computer?
你有使用電腦的經驗嗎？

08 Did any of your previous positions require typing?
你以前的職務中有沒有需要打字的？

209 How many words do you type per minute?
你每分鐘能打多少個字？

210 Have you ever done any correspondence work?
你有處理文書的經驗嗎？

211 Have you ever held a secretarial position?
你曾當過秘書嗎？

212 Do you know how to operate a telephone switchboard?
你會操作電話總機嗎？

213 Do you use a computer?
你會使用電腦嗎？

214 How much experience do you have as a secretary?
你有多少秘書工作經驗？

215 Are you an experienced telephone operator?
你是一個有經驗的接線生嗎？

216 Can you use a typewriter?
你會用打字機嗎？

217 Do you take shorthand?
你會速記嗎？

218 Can you dictate?
你會筆錄嗎？

219 ow did you manage your staff?
你是怎麼管理下屬的？

220 Describe a situation where you had to show leadership.
舉個例說說你是怎樣發揮你的領導才能的？

21 Do you consider your skills above average? About average? Below average?
您覺得自己的技能是優良、一般還是較差？

Answer
·應徵者回答·

22 I could do that with my eyes closed.
我閉著眼睛也能把它做好。

23 I know all the tricks of the trade.
這一行我十八般武藝樣樣精通。

224 I know it like the back of my hand.
我對此瞭如指掌。

225 I wrote the book on that.
我是這方面的權威。

226 I know it backwards and forwards.
我對這個倒背如流。

227 I know it inside and out.
我對這個完全瞭解。

228 I'm an old hand at this.
這方面我可是個老手。

229 Definitely, I'm experienced.
絕對沒有問題，我是老經驗了。

230 I've done it so many times that I could do it blindfolded.
我不知做了多少遍了，現在蒙上眼睛也能做。

231 I'm not a complete novice.
我並非毫無經驗。

232 I am familiar with management.
我熟悉管理。

233 I have a good command of accounting.
我對會計很熟悉。

234 I am quite familiar with western history.
我對西方歷史很熟悉。

235 I am very skillful in operating computers.
我對電腦操作很熟練。

236 I am able to handle the office routines.
我有信心能處理好辦公室例行工作。

237 I have learned to use computers and have become familiar with all clerical duties.
我會使用電腦及熟悉所有文書的工作。

38 I have a good background in standard accounting principles.
我有很好的會計理論基礎。

39 I have worked for the past three years improving my radio engineering knowledge and skills.
過去三年來，我在不斷提高自己在無線電工程方面的知識和技能。

240 I'll bring to a firm foundation of professional knowledge.
我有紮實的專業知識。

241 My interest in the computer goes back to childhood, and I have continued to pursue that interest ever since.
我從小至今一直都對電腦感興趣。

242 My secretarial skills are well above average.
我的秘書技能遠遠高於一般水平。

243 I am experienced in dealing with American clients.
我與美國客戶打交道很有經驗。

244 I have been doing volunteer work for a community center.
我在一家社區中心從事志願服務。

245 My educational background and professional experience make me qualified for the job. Those are you just need.

我的教育背景和工作經驗使我能夠勝任這項工作。那正是你們所需要的。

246 My education and training have given me this useful combination of computer and business.

我所接受的教育和培訓使我能有效地把電腦和商務結合起來。

247 My work required strong mathematics skills and some familiarity with computer networks; however, I never failed to fulfill it satisfactorily.

我所從事的工作對數學能力和電腦網路能力都有很高的要求，但我總能做得令人滿意。

248 I have the ability to plan thoroughly and to implement effectively, the two traits of which are not often found in the same person.

我具備計劃及執行的能力，這兩點都具備的人不多。

249 I have five years experience using a computer.

我有五年使用電腦的經驗。

250 I'm not familiar with computer, but I'm sure I could learn.
我對電腦不太熟悉，不過我相信我一定能夠學得會的。

251 Yes, I've done stenographic work.
是的，我以前做過速記工作。

252 I take shorthand pretty fast.
我的速記寫得很快。

253 I've learned shorthand but have no experience.
我學過速記，不過沒有經驗。

254 I can take dictation.
我可以筆錄。

255 I can type and take dictation.
我可以打字，也可以筆錄。

256 I can take dictation in English at 100 words per minute.
我能用英語筆錄每分鐘100個單字。

257 I can type very quickly.
我打字打得很快。

258 I can type 50 words per minute.
我每分鐘打50個字。

259 I type about 40 words per minute.
我一分鐘大約能打40個字。

260 I can type eighty words per minute.
我一分鐘能打80個字。

261 I can type fast and accurately.
我打字可以又快又準確。

262 I haven't been typing for a year.
If I start it again, it will come back to me.
我一年沒有打字了。
如果我要再打，我馬上就會恢復原來的水準。

263 I type pretty fast but I don't know how many words a minute.
我打得非常的快，不過我不曉得一分鐘打多少字。

264 Yes, typing is my profession line.
是的，打字是我的拿手項目。

65 I've been typing for many years.
我打字打了好多年了。

66 I'm sorry I don't type very well, I can't type fast but I seldom make mistakes.
抱歉，我打得不好，我打得不太快，不過我很難得出錯。

求-職-面-試 小建議

　　關於求職者的工作經驗，企業主最想知道應徵者的工作性質是否與招聘職位相關，及應徵者從以前的工作中吸取到哪些有利的工作經驗。

　　既使過去的工作與申請職位無關，亦不要說自己一無所學，因為每份工作總會有它的可取之處。當被問及對前一個公司的意見時，千萬不要用批評、不滿意的表達方式，因為企業主絕不會喜歡批評前一個公司的員工。

1 實用例句

2 實用會話

3 人事廣告

4 履歷表及自傳

Unit 6 外語能力

Question
・面試官提問・

267 Do you speak a foreign language?
你會講外國語言嗎？

268 How many languages do you speak?
你會講幾種語言？

269 How is your language ability?
你的語言能力怎樣？

270 Do you read and write any other language?
你會讀寫其他語言嗎？

271 Do you speak English?
你會講英語嗎？

272 Can you speak English?
你會講英語嗎？

273 Do you read and write Japanese?
你會讀寫日文嗎？

274 How's your English?
你的英語好不好？

1 實用例句

2 實用會話

3 人事廣告

4 履歷表及自傳

75 How long have you been studying Spanish?
你學西班牙語多久了？

76 How long ago did you start your class in Portuguese?
你多久以前才開始上葡萄牙語課？

277 When did you begin to learn Polish?
你是何時開始學波蘭語的？

278 Why did you study Russian?
你為什麼讀俄語？

279 How come you took English lessons?
你怎麼會學起英文的？

280 Is your English good enough to work in an American firm?
你的英文在美商公司做事夠不夠用？

281 Do you know the language well enough to communicate with English speaking people?
你的(英文)程度和講英語的人交談行不行？

282 Do you think your English is good enough to do desk work?
你想你的英文程度可以做文書工作嗎？

283 What language do you speak other than Chinese?
除了中文之外你還會那國語言？

284 How many languages do you speak?
你會講幾國語言？

285 Can you manage German conversation?
你能用德語談話嗎？

286 Do you think you can make yourself understood in English?
你認為你能用英文表達你的想法嗎？

287 What's your second language in addition to Chinese?
除了中文之外，你的第二語言是什麼？

288 Do you like English? Do you consider yourself strong in English communication?
您喜歡英語嗎？覺得自己的英語溝通能力怎樣？

289 Which band of college English Test have you passed?
大學英語考試過了幾級？

·應徵者回答·

90 I'm bilingual.
我會講兩種語言。

91 I am a linguistic genius.
我有語言天份。

92 I speak English very well.
我英文講得很好。

293 I speak English and German.
我會說英文及德語。

294 I speak French quite fluently.
我講法語相當流利。

295 I speak it well.
我講得很好。

296 I believe my English fluency is quite good.
我認為自己的英語相當流利。

297 I majored in English language so that I could more clearly express my ideas in that language.
我主修的是英語,所以可以清楚的用這種語言表達我的意見。

1 實用例句

2

3

4

298 I would like to practice my English in my work.

我想在工作上多用英語。

299 Other than Chinese, I speak English.
I learned some Spanish in school, but forget all of it.

除了中文之外，我會講英語。
在學校我學過西班牙文，但是現在都忘了。

300 I can communicate with foreigners easily.

我能輕鬆地和外國人溝通。

301 I can speak English as far as foreign languages are concerned.

就外語而言，我說英語說得像外國人。

302 I am quite proficient in both written and spoken French.

我的法語說寫方面相當熟練。

303 Besides Mandarin, my mother tongue, I can also speak English and Japanese.

除了我的母語中文外，我還可以講英語和日語。

304 I have been attending a school to improve my English.

我一直在學校進修英語。

305 I speak the English, French and, of course, Mandarin.

我會講英文、法文和國語。

306 I believe the amount of English I know is sufficient to work in an American firm.

我想我的英語在美商公司做事絕沒問題。

307 I understand English better than I can express myself.

我英文聽的能力比我表達的能力強。

308 I can do both well.

我兩種都會。

309 I only speak the language.

我只會講。

310 I speak the language better than I read and write.

我講的比讀和寫的好。

311 I got a high score on TOEFL.

我托福考試成績很高。

312 Pretty good, I used to be an interpreter in English.

不錯，我以前是英文傳譯員。

313 I've been speaking English all my life.
我講了一輩子的英文了。

314 I can do translation work without difficulties.
我擔任翻譯工作沒有困難。

315 I used to be an interpreter.
我以前做過翻譯員。

316 The amount of English I know enables me to do general deskwork.
我的英語足夠可以做普通文書工作。

317 Because there's a great demand in the world for the usage of English.
因為世界上用英語的地方比較多。

318 Because English is the best language for communication.
因為英文是溝通思想最好的一種語言。

319 English has become an international language. No matter where you go, English is always commonly used, it is convenient to know the language.
英文已經成為一種世界語言。
不論你到那一國去，英文都普遍用得到，如果會英語就方便多了。

320 I began learning English when I was twelve.
我十二歲就開始學英文。

321 I started to learn English when I was in the primary school.
我從小學的時候就開始學英語。

322 I have been learning English for more than ten years.
我英語學了十年以上。

323 I speak the language well.
I've learned ten years of it.
我講得很好。
我學過十年了。

324 I have been studying English since I was in primary school.
我從上小學的時候就學英語。

325 Because I thought if I learned English well, it would help me in getting better jobs.
我想要是我把英文學好了，可以找到比較好的工作。

326 I speak a little bit of everything, but none of them are very good.

我什麼話都會講一點點，可是都不太好。

327 Only enough to carry on a simple conversation.

只可以講簡單會話。

○─○─○ 求-職-面-試 小建議

對於求職應徵者，一般企業主最想知道的是應徵者有沒有擔任該工作的能力。

因此，對於問題應該要誠實回答，例如對方問："Can you manage English conversation？"（你能用英語談話嗎？），應該懂多少便説多少，不要刻意隱瞞自己的缺點而説謊，否則當場或開始就職上班後，還是會露出馬腳的！

Unit 7 工作經歷

Question
面試官提問

328 What have you been doing since your graduation?
自從你畢業以來都在做什麼？

329 What have you been doing since you quit your last job?
你離開前一份工作以後都在做什麼？

330 Do you enjoy your present job?
你喜歡目前的工作嗎？

331 What do you think of your present job?
你認為你目前的工作怎麼樣？

332 How do you like your present job?
你覺得你目前工作如何？

333 Tell me about your last job.
談談你原來的工作。

334 What kind of experience do you have?
你有什麼工作經驗？

335 Could you tell me something about your experience?
能談談你的工作經驗嗎？

336 What kind of work did you do?
你以前做過那一類工作？

337 How did you get to office?
你怎樣去上班的？

338 Would you tell me the general description of your present job?
請你描述一下目前的工作，好嗎？

339 Where were you employed before?
你以前在那裡高就？

340 What did you do in the past?
你過去曾做些什麼事？

341 Would you tell me your employment history?
請你把過去工作經驗告訴我好嗎？

342 Is there a lot of paper work connected with your job?
你的工作是否和文書工作有關？

343 What is your present position with the company?

你目前在公司裏擔任的是什麼職位？

344 What does your work consist of exactly?

你的工作到底都是做些什麼？

345 What's the main part of your job?

你工作最主要部份是什麼？

346 What are your principle responsibilities?

你主要是負責些什麼？

347 What positions have you held before?

你以前擔任過什麼職務？

348 Have you been employed in this field?

你以前在這方面服務過嗎？

349 Have you ever done this kind of work before?

你以前作過這種工作嗎？

350 Have you ever done any work in this field?

你曾經做過這一行業嗎？

351 Are you an experienced telephone operator?

你是一個有經驗的接線生嗎？

352 What have you been doing since you graduate from college?
專科畢業後你都在從事什麼工作？

353 Have you ever done supervisory work?
你是否擔任過管理工作？

354 Do you have any job experience of office work?
你有辦公室工作的經驗嗎？

355 Do you have any experience as a secretary?
你有沒有秘書工作經驗？

356 Do you have any experience as a cashier?
你有沒有收銀員的工作經驗？

357 How much experience do you have as a typist?
你有沒有打字員的工作經驗？

358 Have you got any experience in advertising?
你有廣告方面的經驗嗎？

359 Do you have any sales experience?
你有銷售經驗嗎？

360 Do you have any selling experience?
你有推銷經驗嗎？

361 Have you ever done any selling work?
你曾經擔任過推銷工作嗎？

362 Are you familiar with salesmanship?
你對推銷經驗熟悉嗎？

363 Do you have any experience in doing the job of an editor?
你有沒有從事編輯的經驗？

364 Do you have any experience working overseas?
你有海外工作經驗嗎？

365 Do you have any previous experience of working in the IT industry?
你有IT行業的從業經驗嗎？

366 What supervisory or leadership roles have you had?
你以前做過什麼樣的領導或管理工作？

367 You don't seem to have any experience in sales, do you?
你好像沒有任何銷售經驗，對嗎？

368 Do you have to do a lot of paper work?
你的工作是不是要做很多文書工作？

369 Does your work involve a lot of paper filing
and typing?
你的工作是不是牽涉到很多文件檔案和打字的工
作？

370 Which advertisement company did you serve?
你在哪家廣告公司做事？

371 What kind of position have you held before?
你以前從事過什麼工作？

372 What is your job in the company?
你在那家公司，擔任什麼工作？

373 What kind of experience do you have for the
job?
你有什麼與這份工作相關的經驗？

374 What did you do at CNS?
在CNS你擔任什麼工作？

375 What is your responsibility there?
你在那裡的職責是什麼？

376 What is your biggest accomplishment on the job?

你在工作上最大的成就是什麼？

377 What have you learned from jobs you have held?

你從以往的工作中學到什麼？

378 What did you learned from the last job?

從上一個工作你學到什麼了？

379 What did you accomplish or learn in last job?

你從前一份工作中取得了什麼成就？學到了些什麼？

380 How would you describe your accomplishments in your last job?

在前一份工作中，你取得了什麼成就？

381 What accomplishments have given you most satisfaction?

你取得的什麼成就最令你滿意？

382 What kind of performance reviews did you receive?

你的業績怎樣？老闆是怎樣衡量你的業績的？

383 How do you measure the job performance of your subordinates?

你是怎麼評估下屬的工作業績的？

384 In what areas did your supervisor rate you high and low?

你的上司在哪些方面對您的評估高些？哪些方面是低些？

385 How long have you been working there?

你在那兒工作多久了？

386 86Did you work full time or part time?

你(過去)是專任還是兼任？

387 Have you worked anywhere else?

你在別處工作過嗎？

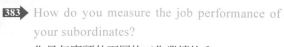
• 應徵者回答 •

388 I have never had a job before.

我以前從未工作過。

389 I have been hunting for a job.

我一直在謀職。

390 I have never had other job.
This is my first time to look for job.
我從來沒有做過事。
這是我第一次找工作。

391 Since I have just graduated from college, I have not had an opportunity to work.
因為我剛大學畢業，尚未工作過。

392 I have never been employed before, because I just finished my study.
我從來沒有做過事，因為我剛離開學校。

393 I have just graduated from college, I hope to look for a job.
我剛大學畢業，希望找份工作做。

394 I have just graduated from college, and I am now looking for a job.
我剛大學畢業，正在謀職。

395 I have had one job since graduating.
畢業後，我曾做過事。

396 I have had two jobs since I left Washington University.
我自華盛頓大學畢業後，曾做過兩份工作。

397 I have been in this field since I graduated from Ohio State University.

俄亥俄州立大學畢業後，我曾在這方面工作過。

398 I work in a library for two years right after college.

我大學畢業就在圖書館做了兩年。

399 When I was in school I was pushing TIME magazine.

我在中學唸書時，就推銷過時代雜誌。

400 On my job I had to work as a switchboard operator.

我上班的時候也要當總機接線生的。

401 I have several years experience as a cashier.

我有好幾年收銀員的經驗。

402 I worked there as an editor.

我在那裡是編輯。

403 I have some experience in secretary.

我有一些做秘書的經驗。

404 I used to be an English teacher.

我過去是一位英文老師。

405 I have been employed as a secretary at a trading company.
我曾在一家貿易公司擔任秘書工作。

406 I am presently working as the personal secretary to the president of BCQ Corporation.
我目前是BCQ公司董事長的私人秘書。

407 I was a secretary for an insurance company.
我在一家保險公司做過秘書。

408 I have been a salesman.
But now, I can do public relations.
我曾做過推銷員工作。
但現在，公共關係我亦能做。

409 I am responsible for the company's correspondence.
我是負責書信撰擬。

410 I have also been a warehouse clerk.
我也曾做過倉庫管理員。

411 I used to be a primary school teacher.
我曾經做過小學教師

412 I am a clerk.
我是辦事員。

413 I was a secretary at Microsoft.
我曾是微軟的秘書。

414 I have both experience in finance and accountancy.
我具有金融和財會兩種工作經驗。

415 I have been an accountant in a trading company.
我一直在一家貿易公司擔任會計工作。

416 I was an export clerk in a foreign trading company.
我曾是一家外商公司的外銷員。

417 I used to work in a publishing company.
我曾在一家出版社工作。

418 I can do all kinds of office work; I hope you could give me the opportunity to work for you.
辦公室各種工作我都能做，希望您能給我一個工作機會。

419 I was in the Sales Department in CNS most of the time.
我在CNS公司，主要在銷售部工作。

20 I was the manager of CSR Department at CNS.
我在CNS公司擔任客戶服務部經理。

21 I can type all kinds of the letter.
我能打各類函件。

22 I started as a receptionist and later promoted as an assistant manager in the sales department.
剛開始我是一名接待員，之後升職做銷售經理助理。

423 I have been the personal secretary to the president of Novell.
我曾擔任過網威董事長私人秘書。

424 I am in charge of the trading department.
我是負責公司貿易部門。

425 I have done this kind of work for several years.
我曾擔任過這類工作好幾年。

426 I have done this type of work before.
我以前曾做過這類工作。

427 I am now assistant manager in the Star Restaurant, in charge of a group of ten.
我現在是星光餐廳的副理，負責十個人的工作。

428 I have received the secretarial training for six months.

我曾接受過六個月的秘書訓練。

429 I worked for five years at an engineering firm.

我在工程公司工作了五年。

430 I have been in the position for two years.

我已經擔任此職位兩年了。

431 I have been a sales manager for the past six years.

過去這六年，我擔任銷售經理一職。

432 I have spent the last four years working specifically in this field.

過去四年我專門在這個領域裡工作。

433 I have been working in an advertisement company in the last two years.

在過去的兩年中，我一直在一家廣告公司工作。

434 For the past three years I've been working for CNS, a New York based Software Company.

過去三年我一直爲CNS公司工作，這是一家紐約的軟體公司。

35 I worked in a shoes shop last summer as a part-time sales girl.

去年夏天時我曾在一家鞋店作兼職售貨員。

36 I was promoted to be the sales manager two years ago.

我在兩年前升遷爲銷售部經理。

37 I have been employed as a program designer in CNS Firm since 2000.

從2000年起，我就在CNS公司做程式設計師。

38 After graduation in 2000 from the English Department of Cornell University, I first taught English at a local high school for three years.

我於2000年從康乃爾大學英語系畢業，接著就在本地一所中學教了三年英語。

39 I have worked at a foreign representative office in New York as an intern for a total of two months during my summer vacation.

我在暑假期間曾在一家外國公司紐約辦事處實習過2個月。

440 I have learned a lot about business know-how and basic office skill.

我學到許多業務訣竅和辦公室基本技能。

441 I have never sold before, but I don't think it's hard to learn.
我從來沒有賣過東西，我覺得也不會太難學。

442 I think I can, I don't mind hard job.
我想我能辦到的，我不怕工作困難。

443 I believe I can do any thing for you.
我相信我能為您做任何事。

444 I have the educational background and relevant experience required by the job.
我有此工作有關的教育及工作經驗。

445 Although the youngest salesperson in the store, I had the second highest sales total.
我雖然是公司年齡最小的銷售員，但我的銷售額卻名列第二。

446 Five years of related work experience, a master's degree in business administration, and strong interpersonal skills have prepared me for a career in office administration.
五年的相關工作經驗，是工商企業管理碩士，人際交流溝通能力強，我能勝任高級管理工作。

47 My experience, particularly my work with Oracle, is strong preparation for your advertised position.

我的經歷，尤其是在甲骨文的那一段經歷，為我應聘貴公司的職位做了準備。

48 Having worked for three years as a part-time journalist for a local newspaper, I've gained a great deal of practical knowledge in all aspects of society.

我曾為本地的一家報社當過三年的兼職記者，獲得了豐富的社會知識。

49 I have completed a Master's Degree in English, taught Business Communication at major university, worked for two newspapers.

我取得了英語碩士學位，在一所重點大學教過商業通信課程，在兩家報社任職過。

50 I am confident that this experience would help me fit in and contribute to the work in your company.

我深信，這段經歷使我能適合貴公司的工作，並在工作中做出貢獻。

451 I believe my background would benefit your company.

我相信，我的經歷和能力對貴公司會很有用的。

452 I believe that my background, experience, and education have given me the unique qualifications for the position.

我相信，憑我的經驗、學歷和能力，完全能勝任這份工作。

453 That experience taught me to manage my time, so you'll find me a very efficient time budgeter as well as a competent financial budgeter.

那段經歷教會了我該怎樣使用時間，所以，您會發現，我不但是個合格的財務規劃的人，而且是個高效率的時間安排者。

454 Although I have no experience in this field, I am willing to learn.

雖然我在這方面沒有經驗，但是我願意去學習。

455 I am sorry to say that I have no experience in this field.

很抱歉，我在這方面毫無經驗。

56 No, but I know the duties that a secretary has and believe I can accomplish the duties.

沒有，不過我曉得一個秘書應該做的事情，我覺得我可以勝任這份工作。

57 Yes, I have done that kind of work.

是的，我做過這一類的工作。

58 Yes, I have experience at that.

是的，我有這種經驗。

59 No, but I'm willing to learn

沒有做過，不過我很願意學習。

60 No, I have never done this work before, but I will try very hard.

沒有，我以前從未做過這類工作，但是我願意去試一試。

61 I often work overtime at night.

我經常在夜間工作。

Unit 8 工作內容

Question
面試官提問

462 How much do you know about this job?
你對這份工作有多了解？

463 The position is assistant to the sales manager.
這個工作是協助銷售部經理的工作。

464 The job is highly demanding, both physically and mentally.
這個工作在體力和精神力上都要求很高。

465 It's not as easy as it seems.
它不像乍看上去那麼容易。

466 It's harder than it looks.
它比看上去的要難。

467 It's a real challenge for us.
這對於我們是一個挑戰。

468 New employees here often have a punishing workload.
這兒的新雇員經常需要超負荷工作。

9 Fishing for and keeping big customers is a tricky business.

找到並且保住大客戶是一門學問。

0 Finding the solution to this perennial problem is not an easy task.

為這個大難題找到解決辦法可不是件容易的事。

71 Now we face the daunting task of clearing up the mess.

現在我們得做一件費力氣的事情：收拾爛攤子。

72 It requires working odd hours and is very demanding.

有時需加班，工作很重。

73 What would be your response if we put you in Sales Department?

如果我們派你去行銷部工作你願意嗎？

74 I hope you will be happy working with our firm.

我希望你在我們公司裡工作愉快。

75 We need someone there rather urgently.

我們那裡非常缺人。

Answer
應徵者回答

476 There is too much paper work to do.
文書方面的事太多了。

477 My jobs are taking dictation and typing letters.
我的工作是做筆錄和打信。

478 My main job is overseeing a large department store.
我主要工作是管理一個大百貨公司

479 I'm handling invoices, shipping bills and computing freight costs; that is most of the documentation.
我管發票、發貨單和估計運費的事；其實也就是文書方面的事情。

480 My main responsibility is troubleshooting between top management and the general employees.
我的主要職務是解決行政方面與員工間的問題。

481 Would you be able to describe a typical day on the job?
你能描述一下這個職位的日常工作內容嗎？

82 I received continuous promotions as result of my efficient performance of duties and my skill in working with people.

我出色地履行了我的職責，善於與人合作，因此不斷受到提拔。

83 What level of responsibility could I expect in this position?

假如從事這份工作，我會承擔多大的職責？

84 Is there a typical career path for a person in this position?

這份工作有沒有固定的生涯發展？

485 What are the company's working hours?

公司的上下班時間是怎樣的？

486 Would I have to work overtime very often?

是否要經常加班？

487 Would there be any opportunities to work abroad in the future?

將來有機會到國外工作嗎？

488 If you will give me a try, I'm sure I'll start to pick things up.

您要是給我機會試一試的話，我想我一定會學會的。

489 I think I can, I don't mind hard work.
我想我可以的，我不怕苦。

490 I've never done that before, but I'll try very hard.
我以前從來沒有做過那種工作，不過我會盡量努力。

491 I expect to work hard, Mr. Brown.
布朗先生，我早知道工作會艱苦的。

492 I like being on the road.
我喜歡在外面跑。

493 I don't mind being away for a day or two at a time, but I don't like long trips.
要是每次離開家一兩天倒是沒有什麼關係，我不願意出差太久。

494 I would rather not travel, but if it is required, and the trips are short, I'd go.
我不願意出差，不過要是非去不可而且路途不太遠的話，我也可以。

495 I enjoy traveling; I would be even happier to accept a job involving traveling.
我喜歡出差。如果要是經常出差，那最合我的意。

96 What do you see as the priorities for someone in this position?
你在招聘這個職位時優先考慮哪些條件？

97 How are employees evaluated and promoted?
公司如何評價和提拔職員？

98 What training programs do you have available for your employees?
公司有什麼樣的雇員培訓計劃？

499 What are the company's plans for the future?
公司未來的發展方向是什麼？

500 On the average, I work six hours overtime a week.
平均，我一個星期加六小時班。

501 My boss requires overtime work, but there is often a handsome bonus for this.
我的老板常常叫我們加班，可是加班費也相當不錯。

502 I am not afraid of hard work; in fact, I enjoy it.
我不怕工作辛苦，實際上，我喜歡艱苦的工作。

Unit 9 工作期望

503 What are your short-term goals?
你的短期目標是什麼？

504 What would you like to be doing in five years?
Ten years?
你五年後的目標是什麼？十年後的目標又是什麼？

505 What would you like to be doing two years
from now?
二年後你希望自己在做什麼？

506 Where do you see yourself in two years?
你覺得二年後的自己會如何？

507 What did you learn or gain from your part-time
experiences?
從打工經驗中，你學到了什麼？

508 What did you like most about your job? What
did you like least?
這份工作你最喜歡的是什麼？最不喜歡什麼？

09 Describe your career, its progression, and what you have accomplished.
What are your future plans?
談談您的工作情況、工作進展和成就。
還有您將來有什麼計畫？

10 What is the most important thing you are looking for in an employer?
你在找工作時，最期待雇主哪一種特質？

11 What experience have you had working on a team?
你有怎樣的團隊工作經驗？

12 What do you consider important when looking for a job?
你選擇工作時主要的考慮是什麼？

13 What do you think you would bring the job?
你認為你將能為這份工作帶來什麼？

14 How long do you plan to stay with this company, if hired?
如果被雇用，你打算在這家公司待多久？

15 What are you looking for in your next job?
你希望在下一份工作內得到什麼？

516 What is your career objective?
你的事業目標是什麼？

517 What kind of working conditions do you like best?
您理想的工作環境是什麼？

518 Do you have any idea how long you plan to stay here?
你打算在這裡待多久呢？

519 How long do you want to stay here?
你打算在這裡待多久？

520 What ideas do you have if we employ you?
如果我們錄用你，你有什麼想法？

521 Do you mind if you have to go to other countries a lot?
你會介意如果經常要去其他國家出差嗎？

522 You will have to travel frequently if you accept this position.
你要是接受這個職位的話，你得要經常出差的。

523 Would you mind working on weekends?
週末加班你會介意嗎？

24 Would you mind working overtime at night?
如果有夜間加班，你會介意嗎？

25 This job is not in Taipei, are you willing to work in other places?
這份工作地點不在台北，你願不願意到其他地方去工作？

26 You'll be on the road a lot if you take this job. Is that satisfactory?
假如你要接受這份工作，你大部份的時間都要在外面跑，這樣子你覺得可以嗎？

27 This job opening is not in this city.
Are you willing to work in places other than Taipei?
這個工作不是在台北市。
你願意在別的地方工作嗎？

28 You will be put on probation during your training period, which means you employment may be terminated at any time until you have completed the program and we feel that your are competent.
在你接受訓練的這段期間算是試用階段，那意思就是說，在你受訓結束之前，你可能隨時被解聘。

529 I think I am an excellent match for this job.
我認為我恰好適合這個職位。

530 I feel I am ready for a more challenging position.
我認為我有能力承擔更具挑戰性的工作。

531 I'd like to find a job which is more challenging.
我希望做一個更有挑戰性的工作。

532 I would like to get a more specialized job.
我想獲得一份更加專業化的工作。

533 I can hit the ground running.
我能夠馬上進入工作狀態。

534 I've been looking for the job of an editor.
我一直都在尋找編輯的工作。

535 I am confident I can be a competent editor.
我深信自己能成為一個稱職的編輯。

536 I've been looking for the job you offer.
我一直都在尋找你們提供的這種工作。

537 I have always wanted to be a reporter.
記者是我一直夢寐以求的工作。

538 I hope to have a job, which offers me an opportunity for advancement.
我希望有一個提供我升遷機會的工作。

539 I wish to move up to higher position with acquisition of more experience in the future.
我希望將來的職位隨著我工作經驗的增加而逐步提升。

540 I hope I could be a leader of an energetic and productive sales team.
我希望成為一支有活力及高生產率的銷售團隊的主管。

541 I expect to operate computers.
我希望操作電腦。

542 I'd rather work in the business department if choices may be given.
如果可以選擇，我願意在營業部工作。

543 This job is good for me to develop some of the things I've learned in my major.
這份工作能對我在學校學的東西有所發展。

544 I think hotel industry is the right career for me.
我認為飯店業對我非常合適。

545 What I really want is the chance to learn some advanced methods of management from foreign staff members.
我真正希望的是要從外國職員那裡學到一些先進的管理方法。

546 I speak fairly good English and I enjoy meeting different kinds of people, so I think I could handle the work of a receptionist.
我能說流利的英語，而且我喜歡接觸不同的人，所以我認為我能勝任接待員一職。

547 Banking is the kind of work I want to do and that city bank is the one in which I would like to work.
銀行業是我想從事的行業，花旗銀行正是我想工作的銀行。

548 I could immediately put my excellent training and extensive knowledge to work for your company.
我受過良好的培訓，有廣博的知識，能馬上為貴公司服務。

549 I feel that my academic background and my work experience qualify me for this position.

憑我的學歷和工作經歷，完全能勝任該職位。

550 I have developed a habit of devoting all of my energy to every job project.

我養成了這樣的習慣，能全神貫注地學習和工作。

551 I know that you do a very big international business, so I thought it would be a good place for me to make use of the experience I have had abroad.

我知道貴公司在國際貿易工作方面的生意做得很大，所以，我想這裡會是運用我在國外獲得的經驗的好地方。

552 I plan to leave the present job in order to be able to get into the advertising business.

我計劃離開目前的工作是為了進入廣告業務以尋求發展。

553 My internship at CNS Industries proved my competency for challenging jobs.

我在CNS實業公司的實習證明，我能勝任頗具挑戰性的工作。

554 I'm looking for a permanent job with promotions and raises.

我在找一個固定的職業，將來能夠有升遷或者加薪的機會。

555 I am sure that I could do the work well, I also feel that I have the necessary qualifications.

我相信我可以勝任，我覺得你所需要的條件我都夠。

556 Are you looking for a dynamic salesperson?

你們需要充滿活力的銷售人員嗎？

557 I would like to contribute my skills to your company's development.

希望能用我的知識和技能為貴公司的發展做出貢獻。

558 My business experience, experience in using computers, and communication skills qualify me to be an effective part of the sales staff at CNS.

我的商務經歷、電腦使用經歷以及溝通技能使我能成為CNS公司的一位優秀的銷售人員。

559 Within a short period of time, I can perform effectively as one of your staff members.
我在短期間內，就能成爲貴公司一位優秀的職員。

560 I think my education as well as my professional experience will be well appropriate for the position.
我相信，憑我的學歷和工作經驗，完全能勝任該職位。

561 However, they were similar and I'm willing to learn.
雖然如此，可是我這些經驗是極其相似的，而且我願意學習。

562 Frankly, I'm well qualified for this position. Hopefully, you are willing to give me a probation work period to prove myself.
老實的講，這份工作我是足夠資格的。
只希望你同意給我一段試用期來證明我自己。

563 The first day it might be new, but I learn quickly and I know I can handle the job.
第一天可能會生疏，不過我學得很快，我知道我可以勝任的。

564 I like to work with people who are honest, dedicated to their work.

我喜歡與一些誠實並對工作投入的人合作。

565 I hope to have a job which offers me an opportunity for advancement.

我希望有一個提供升級機會的工作。

566 This job you offer is more interesting to me than any salary you may offer.

Happiness in my work is most important to me.

您這裏的這份工作對我來說比您所給的薪水還有興趣。

工作有沒有意思對我是非常重要的。

567 I believe the course in market research I have taken will help me to make an impressive contribution to your market development.

我相信，我所學的市場調查方面的課程，能使我爲貴公司的市場開拓做出巨大的貢獻。

568 As scholarship-winning student of English major and Chinese minor, I believe my skills as a public relations practitioner would be a useful attribute in your public affairs department.

我主修英語，輔修中文，獲得過獎學金，具有一定的公關能力，能爲貴公司的公共關係發展做出貢獻。

569 I believe my experience in taxation as well as my familiarity with the local business community would enable me to contribute to your firm's needs.

我熟悉本地商務情況，又有稅收方面的經歷，能夠爲貴公司做出貢獻。

570 I have been getting ready to go abroad to America.

我一直都在準備著去美國。

571 I've been gaining practical experience in the import/export business.

我一直在學進出口生意。

572 What qualities do you look for in new employees?

你希望新員工具備哪些條件？

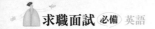
573 I am not familiar with the nature of the job, nor with your company policy, so I don't dare make any statement.

我既不熟識工作性質，也不瞭解貴公司的政策，所以，我不敢發表任何意見。

求-職-面-試 小建議

　　別因為想短時間內找到工作，就對所有的工作提出申請。

　　應先自我衡量此工作是否真是自己想要得到的工作，別用「騎驢找馬」的心態隨便接受工作，否則一旦開始工作後才發現並非符合自己的期望，只好離職繼續找下一份工作，工作經驗不但不容易累積，幾年後你會發現，自己仍是一事無成地四處找工作！

Unit 10 薪資

Question
面試官提問

574 What salary would you expect to get?
你希望拿多少薪水？

575 What is your monthly salary?
你的月薪有多少？

576 How much money are you making a month?
你一個月賺多少錢？

577 What are your salary expectations?
你的希望薪資是多少？

578 What salary do you expect per month?
你要求多少月薪？

579 What salary do you expect per year?
你要求多少年薪？

580 What salary do you want?
你要求多少薪資？

581 What pay do you expect?
你希望工資是多少？

582 What is the lowest salary you may consider?
最低多少薪水，你才可以考慮？

583 What is your expected salary?
你希望多少薪水？

584 What salary are you looking for?
你想要多少新資？

585 How much money are you looking for in this job?
你希望這個工作的薪水是多少？

586 What is your asking price?
你要求的薪水是多少？

587 Are you paid on a commission or salary basis?
你是拿薪水的，還是拿佣金的？

588 What salary were you earning?
你當時的工資是多少？

589 How much money are you presently earning?
你目前賺多少？

590 How much do you make at your current job?
你目前的工作薪資是多少？

591 How about your present pay?
你目前的薪水是多少？

592 How much money do you get now?
你目前薪資是多少？

593 What is your monthly salary now?
你目前的月薪是多少？

594 What starting salary would you expect here?
你期望在這裡起薪多少？

595 Would you expect an increase in your present salary?
你是否期望比目前的薪水高一些？

596 Would you mind if the starting salaries are quite low and there is a three-month period on probation?
如果起薪很低，並且還有三個月的試用期你介意嗎？

597 This job offers you $5,000 a month plus room and board, would you be interested?
這份工作是一個月 5 千元，包括食住，你有興趣嗎？

598 This job offers you $5,000 a month. Would you be interested?

這份工作是一個月 5 千元，你對它有興趣嗎？

599 I believe we can offer you 2,500 dollars a month at the start.
Would that be satisfactory?

我想我們可以給你每個月 2500 元的起薪。
你覺得滿意嗎？

600 An average accountant earns about $10,000 a month.

一般的會計大概每月可拿一萬元。

601 Would you consider a starting salary at twenty-two hundred?

起薪 2200 你要不要考慮？

602 The starting salary should be least $2,000 per month.

起薪最低應該至少每月 2 千元。

603 That's a little more than we had planned.

這比我們計劃的多了一些。

604 Work on weekends should be paid.

週末加班應該付報酬。

05 The salary per month is US$3,000.

月薪是美金三千元。

06 The starting salary is not very high, because this is a new company.

因為本公司是新公司，故起薪並不很高。

07 The starting salary is not high, but the fringe benefits are many and there will be many opportunities for advancement.
Both your position and salary will be reconsidered after only six months.

剛開始薪水不會太高，不過福利很多，同時升遷的機會也多。
過了六個月後你的職位和薪水都可能會調整的。

08 Since you have just graduated and are inexperienced in this field, we can only offer you $3,000 a month to start. However, if you do well we will give you raises to commensurate with your ability.

因為你剛剛畢業，而且在這一方面又沒有經驗，我們一開始只能一個月給你三千元。可是呢，你要是做得好，我們會按照你的才能給你加薪。

1 實用例句

2

3

4

Answer
• 應徵者回答 •

609 I am hunting for a job of higher wages.
我正想找一份薪水高的工作。

610 Based on my skills and experience, I am looking for four thousand a month.
根據我的能力和經驗，我希望月薪是 4000 元。

611 As for salary, I leave it to you to decide after experience of my capacity.
至於薪水，還是等檢驗了我的能力之後由你們再作決定吧。

612 I think you'll find I'm worth it.
我想你會發現我值得拿那些錢。

613 Although my present job is good for me, the salary is too low to support my family.
雖然我目前的工作很好，但薪水太低，無法維持家庭。

614 I hope to make 50,000 a month for supporting my family.
為了維持家庭，我希望一個月賺 5 萬元。

615 I'm presently making seven thousand a month.
我目前的薪水是一個月 7000 元。

16 My present monthly salary is 5000, insurance and bonus not included.

I don't think the salary here is lower than that, isn't it?

我目前的月薪是 5000 元，不包括保險和獎金。

我想這兒的工資不會比那低吧，對嗎？

17 One good qualified man is better than a score of men.

I can handle this work easily by myself and you'll end up saving money if you pay me ten thousand a month.

一個有能力的人比一大堆沒用的人強。

這個工作我一個人就可以做，你要是給我一個月一萬元的話，結果你反而省錢。

18 After taxes, my take home pay is over US $20,000 a year.

付稅以後，我每年淨拿兩萬美元以上。

19 As a salesman I am paid a basic salary plus a sales commission.

因為我是推銷員，我有一個固定的底薪，另外加上佣金。

20 I'm looking for eight thousand a month.

我希望月薪是 8000 元。

621 I'm asking in the five thousand a month.
我要求月薪是5000元。

622 I'd like one million dollars a year.
我想要年薪100萬元。

623 My expected minimum salary is five thousand a month.
我希望的最低工資是每月5000元。

624 I'm making $2,500 a month.
我一個月2500元。

625 Would you tell me your salary practice?
請告訴我貴公司的薪資情況，好嗎？

626 What are your performance incentives and the bonus structure?
你們的獎勵、獎金系統是怎樣的？

627 What pay will I get?
我的薪水是多少呢？

628 I don't mind the salary.
我不在乎薪水的多少。

29 I'd like my monthly salary to be thirty thousand plus 2% commission on all sales.
我希望月薪30,000元，另加銷售額2％的佣金。

30 I'd require a commencing salary of 50,000 a month.
我要求起薪每月五萬元。

31 I'd agree to have a trial period and then adjust my salary according to my competence.
我同意試用一段時間，然後根據我的工作表現調整薪資。

32 I don't mind starting from a lower salary if I only know there're chances for advancements, then I can always live on hopes.
開始的時候薪水低不要緊，假如要是有升遷的機會的話，我總可以有個希望。

33 I think we can reach an agreement on the salary if I can be sure that there's a good chance to advance in this company.
假如我要是能夠曉得在這個公司裏工作有升遷的機會的話，薪水好解決。

634 I don't mind if I start with a low salary because the experience I have had was not with a publishing.

一開始的時候，薪水低倒不要緊，因為我的經驗並不是出版界的經驗。

635 I'm quite satisfied with the salary. That would be more than I have expected.

我很滿意薪資，比我期望的要多。

636 That would be quite satisfactory.

我非常的滿意。

637 I'd rather leave that to you, Mr. Jones.

瓊斯先生，這個還是由您決定好了。

638 That's fine with me.

我沒有問題。

639 No problem for me.

對我來說，毫無問題。

640 I thought the salary is too low.

我認為這個薪資實在太少了。

41 I would expect the standard rate of pay at your company for a person with my experiences and educational background.

我希望是貴公司對一個具有我這種經驗和教育背景的人，所付的標準薪資。

42 I'll leave it to you, for I'm not in the position to ask for a certain salary.

關於這件事，就由你來決定好了，因為我沒有資格來講一定要多少薪資。

43 I know little about your salary scale.

我不大知道你們這兒的薪資標準。

44 Since this will be my first job and I lack experience, I hesitate to suggest a salary.

因為這是我頭一次在外面工作，而且我又沒有經驗我不願意談多少薪水。

45 When will we get a raise?

我們何時才會加薪?

Unit 11 福利

646 How about the benefits?
有沒有什麼福利？

647 What is your benefit policy?
你們的福利政策是什麼？

648 Could you give me a full detail of it?
能否詳細告訴我細節？

649 Any other welfare packages for the first three months?
前三個月有沒有其他的什麼福利？

650 We have all the fringe benefits, too.
我們還提供附加的員工福利。

651 We offer an excellent compensation and benefits package including a 5-day week, medical scheme, purchase discounts.
我們提供良好的薪金及福利，包括週休 2 日、醫療規劃、員工購物折扣優惠。

52 We offer competitive salary, stock sharing, project bonus, and moderate training, certification training... .

本公司提供有競爭力的薪資、員工認股、企業紅利、基本培訓、認證培訓等。

53 We offer attractive compensation package, excellent working environment.

For the right people, our growing organization offers plenty of career opportunities.

我們提供極具吸引力的競爭性薪資、良好的工作環境。

對於合適的人選而言，我們日益成長的組織機構提供了大量就業機會。

54 This job occasionally involves some traveling.

We give you allowance for all traveling expenses.

這個工作中間需要你出差旅行。

我們會負擔一切開支及旅行費用的。

55 5 working days per week, 12 days of annual holiday per year, 13 months of salary is fixed, extra bonus can be expected.

每週週休 2 日、一年 12 天年假、13 月薪資，並另有紅利。

656 The medical insurance is necessary.
會有醫療保險。

657 There is a two-month vacation each year.
有兩個月的年假。

658 Your starting pay is \$2,000 a month, for women there is a one-day sick leave a month or twelve days a year.
你一開始是一個月兩千元，女職員每一個月可以請一天病假，或者按年請十二天假也可以。

659 Your salary is US\$ 4000 per month, in addition to insurance and bonuses.
你的工資是每月美金 4,000 元，另加保險和獎金。

Unit
12 離職

60 Why did you quit?
你為什麼要離職？

61 Could you tell me why you want to leave your present job?
能告訴我你為什麼想辭去目前的工作？

62 Why are you leaving your present job?
你為什麼要放棄目前的工作？

63 Why are you leaving your present place of employment?
你為何要離開你目前的工作呢？

64 Why do you want to look for another job?
你為何要去找另外的工作？

65 What made you decide to change job?
是什麼使你決定更換工作？

66 Why did you leave?
你為什麼離開（工作）？

667 Why did you leave that job?
你爲什麼辭掉那份工作？

668 Why do you plan to leave the present job?
你爲什麼打算離開現在的工作？

669 Why do you want to leave your current employment?
你爲什麼希望離開目前的工作？

670 When did you left there?
你什麼時候離開那裡的？

671 What was your reason for leaving?
你離開的原因爲何呢？

672 How long did you work there and why did you leave?
你在那裡工作多久，爲什麼要離開？

673 When did you start work there and when did you leave?
你什麼時候在那裡工作，何時離開的？

674 How do you feel about your former employer?
您覺得前一個雇主如何？

75 Does your present employer know that you are leaving him?
你目前的老板知道你要離開他嗎？

76 What's the reason why you left your previous employer?
你離開原來那個雇主的原因是什麼？

77 Why do you want to change your job?
為什麼你想轉換工作？

78 Why do you want to resign your position as secretary?
你為什麼想辭去秘書的職務？

579 How long did you work at each job?
你的每一份工作做了多久？

580 Why were you out of work for so long?
你為何這麼久沒有工作？

581 How many places have you worked altogether?
你一共工作了幾個地方？？

682 What made you change your job so frequently?
為什麼你經常換工作？

683 So, you were fired?
所以，你是被炒魷魚了？

684 Where are your previous places of
employment?
你以前的工作地點在那裡？

Answer
•應徵者回答•

685 I was fired.
我被開除。

686 I had a lay-off.
我被資遣了。

687 That job was not challenging enough.
那份工作挑戰性不高。

688 The work is not bad. But the salary is too small.
那份工作倒是不錯，但是薪水太少了。

689 I liked the work.
However, the firm is too small for me to widen
my experience.
我喜歡那份工作。
但那家公司太小了，難以增加我的工作經驗。

90 I don't find it too interesting; it offers too little challenge.

我的工作很乏味，它缺乏挑戰性。

91 The work is out of my field.

我的工作跟我所學的不一樣。

92 I'd like to work somewhere closer to my house.

我喜歡離家近一點的工作。

93 Management changed and we did not get along.

經理換人，而我們又處不來。

594 To speak frankly, I did not enjoy that work very much.

坦率地說，我不是很喜歡那份工作。

595 I am working in a small company where further promotion is impossible.

我在一家小公司工作，所以晉升不大可能。

696 I would like to have a job that is more lively than my present one.

因為我希望找到一份較有活力的工作。

697 They let me go.
Because I did not agree with their business philosophy.
他們讓我走。
因為我不同意他們的經營理念。

698 I am capable of more responsibilities, so I decided to change my job.
我完全能夠承擔更多的責任,所以我決定換工作。

699 My present employer does not know I'm leaving.
我現在的老板不知道我要離職。

Unit 13 基本問題

Question
・面試官提問・

10 How old are you ?
你多少歲？

11 Where are you from?
你來自哪裏？

12 Are you a local resident?
你是本地人嗎？

13 Where is your birthplace?
你的出生地在哪裏？

14 What is your date of birth?
你出生年月日是哪一天？

15 How tall are you?
你身高多少？

16 Have you started a family?
你成家了嗎？

17 How many are there in your household?
你家有幾口人？

708 Who are the members of your family?
你家有誰？

709 Do you have (any) children?
你有小孩嗎？

710 How many children do you have?
有多少孩子？

711 Do you have a large family?
你的家人多不多？

712 How many persons are there in your family?
你家裡有幾口人？

713 How many dependents do you have?
有多少家眷？

714 Are you married/single?
你已婚／單身嗎？

715 Have you ever been married?
你以前結過婚嗎？

716 Is your wife working?
你的太太在工作嗎？

17 Where and what kind of work does your wife do?

你的太太在哪裏？做什麼樣的工作。

18 What does your husband do?

你先生做什麼？

19 What is your husband's occupation?

你先生的職業是什麼？

20 What kind of business is your husband in ?

你先生是做什麼生意？

21 Do you live far from here?

你住得遠嗎？

22 What kind of occupation does your father do?

你的父親做什麼職業？

23 How many brothers and sisters do you have ?

你有幾個兄弟和姊妹？

24 Can you drive?

你會開車嗎？

25 Do you ride (drive) a motorcycle?

你會騎摩托車嗎？

726 How will you get to work each day?
你每天怎麼來上班呢?

727 How do you get to work?
你怎樣去上班?

728 What time do you go to work?
你幾點鐘去上班?

729 What time does your work start?
你幾點鐘開始上班?

730 What time do you leave the office?
你幾點離開辦公室?

731 What time does the office close?
你們公司幾點關門?

732 How do you get home?
你怎樣回家?

733 How do you get to work and get home?
你怎樣上下班?

Answer
·應徵者回答·

34 I am twenty-three years old.
我廿三歲。

35 I just turned twenty-two last Tuesday.
我上星期二剛滿廿二。

36 I was born on April eleventh, 1966.
我生於一九六六年四月十一日。

37 I'm from Taipei.
我來自台北。

38 I'm a local resident.
我是本地人。

39 I was born in Taipei.
我生在台北。

40 I was born in Buffalo, America.
我在美國水牛城出生。

41 There's no hurry for that, I think I'll try to earn
enough for that.
用不著忙，我想先試著多賺一些錢再說。

742 Yes, sir, I'm married.
是的，先生，我結婚了。

743 No, sir, I'm still single.
沒有，先生，我還是單身。

744 I'm planning to get married next month.
我打算下個月結婚。

745 No, I don't want to settle down yet.
沒有，我還不想安定下來。

746 He is in the import/export business.
他做進出口生意。

747 He's out of work right now, because he's recovering from a car accident.
他目前沒有工作，因為車禍在休養中。

748 She is not working.
The children keep her busy enough.
她沒做事。
孩子們已經使她夠忙了。

749 She's a retired school teacher.
她是退休的小學老師。

30 He works for the government.
他是公務員。

31 Altogether there are four in my family.
我家一共有四人。

32 My parents, three brothers and two sisters.
我有雙親、三個兄弟和兩個姊妹。

33 Our family consists of my father, my mother, two brothers and me.
我家裏有父親、母親、兩個兄弟還有我。

34 My husband, our two children.
我的先生，兩個孩子。

35 No, we don't have any children.
沒有，我們沒有孩子。

36 One is on the way.
一個快要生了。

37 Yes, I have three sons. They are all abroad.
我有三個兒子，都在國外。

58 I have a five-year old girl.
我有個五歲的女兒。

759 I don't have anyone.
I am a single.
我家沒有任何人。
我是單身。

760 My father is a retired civil servant.
我的父親是一個退休公務員。

761 My father just passed away two months ago.
我的父親前二個月才過世了。

762 My father runs an import and export company.
我的父親經營一家進出口公司。

763 I went to the office by bus everyday.
我每天搭公共汽車上班的

764 Yes, I can drive. I have driven a car for seven years.
我會開車，我已經開車開了七年了。

765 I have a license to drive a motorcycle.
我有機車的駕駛執照。

766 I will ride my motorcycle to work each day.
我每天會騎摩托車來上班的。

57 I ride the bus.
我搭乘巴士。

58 I catch a train to my office.
我搭火車去公司。

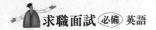
Unit 14 人格特質

Question
•面試官提問•

769 What kind of personality do you think you have?
你認為你具有哪種性格？

770 What is the most important thing for you to be happy?
你認為對你來說，幸福最重要的是什麼？

771 What basic principles do you apply to your life?
你生活中的基本原則是什麼？

772 What are your weak points?
你的缺點是什麼？

773 Can you work under pressure?
你能在壓力下工作嗎？

774 What are your strengths and weaknesses?
您的優點和缺點是什麼？

75 What are your strengths (weaknesses)?
你的優點（缺點）是什麼？

76 What is your greatest strength (weakness)?
您最大的優點(弱點)是什麼？

77 What do you consider your strengths (weaknesses)?
你認為你的長處（缺點）是什麼？

778 Tell me about your weaknesses (strengths).
告訴我你的缺點（優點）。

779 What adjectives would you use to describe yourself?
您覺得用哪些形容自己最恰當？

780 Do you think you are introverted or extroverted?
你認為自己的性格是內向還是外向？

781 Are you an introvert or an extrovert?
你是內向型還是外向型的人？

782 What kind of person do you think you are?
你認為你是哪類人？

783 Would you describe yourself as outgoing or more reserved?
你認為你是個外向的還是個內向的人？

784 What kind of people do you like to work with?
你最喜歡和哪類人合作？

785 How do you get along with others?
你與別人相處如何？

786 How do you deal with those who you think are difficult to work with?
你怎樣應付哪些你認為難以合作的人？

Answer
•應徵者回答•

787 I'm very organized and extremely capable.
我非常有組織能力，也很能幹。

788 I have strong organizational skills.
我的組織能力很強。

789 I'm inclined to think independently.
我喜歡獨立思考問題。

790 I'm quite active and energetic.
我積極而充滿活力。

791 My strong sense of cooperation and intense kindness to people would fit me harmoniously into your organization.

我有很強的合作意識，對人友好，能和貴公司的員工融洽相處。

792 I'm a good team player.

我是一個富有團隊精神的人。

793 I think I'm a cooperative worker.

我認為我具有合作精神。

794 I'm afraid I'm a poor talker.

我這個人恐怕不善言談。

795 I think I am rather outgoing.

I enjoy working with others. But sometimes I want to be alone.

我想我較外向。

我喜歡和別人合作，不過有時我也想一個人獨處。

796 I'm afraid I'm a poor talker, and that's not very good, so I've been learning how to speak in public.

我這個人恐怕不善言談，這樣不好，所以我一直在學習怎樣在眾人面前講話。

797 I wouldn't call myself introverted though sometimes I'm reserved and enjoy staying all by myself, often and often I like sharing activities with others.

我不算內向，儘管有時我沉默寡言，喜歡獨處，但我喜歡和其他人一起活動。

798 Sometimes I lack patience in what I am doing. However, I'm very careful with my work.

我有時候對自己的所作所為缺乏耐心。
不過，我工作挺細心。

799 I'm a fast-learner.

我學東西很快。

800 I am anxious to learn and hope for an opportunity to demonstrate my ability.

我渴望學習，希望能有機會展示我的才能。

801 I learn fast, I remember what I learn, and most important of all, I can apply what I learn to work and make great achievements.

我學得快，記得快，能把學到的用於工作，取得較大的成就。

802 You will find that I am most eager to learn and very happy when I keep busy.

您會發現，我渴望學習，喜歡忙碌，並以此為樂。

803 I shall bring to the job a willingness to work and an eagerness to improve.
Let me prove this to you.

我樂於學習，渴望進步。
希望能有機會向您證實。

804 There will be many routines and procedures that will be new to me.
You will find me eager to learn and to improve.

我有許多新東西需要學習。
我也樂於學習，渴望進步。

805 I pride myself on my punctuality, accuracy, and dependability.

我準時守信、精益求精，而且值得信任。

806 I stick to my principles and keep to rule.

我會堅持原則和謹守規則。

807 I approach things enthusiastically and I don't like leaving things half done.

我熱誠對待每件事，不喜歡半途而廢。

 實用例句 ①

實用會話 ②

人事廣告 ③

履歷表及自傳 ④

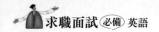

808 I am a hard worker when I have something challenging to do.
我在遇到挑戰性的工作時，我是個很努力的人。

809 I'm a hard-working, persistent person.
我是工作刻苦，性情執著的人。

Unit 15 休閒生活

Question
・面試官提問・

810 What do you most enjoy doing outside of working hours-hobbies and other activities?
您不工作的時間喜歡做些什麼？有什麼興趣愛好？還參加些什麼活動？

811 What do you do in your spare time?
你在工作之餘時，有何消遣呢？

812 Do you have any hobbies?
你有什麼嗜好呢？

813 What are your hobbies?
你的嗜好是什麼？

814 What do you like to do?
你喜歡做什麼？

815 What do you like to do during holiday?
在假日，你喜歡做些什麼？

816 What do you do in your leisure time?
你平時休閒時間會做什麼消遣？

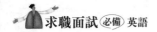
817 How do you spend your leisure time?
你是如何打發業餘時間的？

818 What do you do when you are not working?
工作之餘你有什麼消遣活動？

819 What kind of sports do you like?
你喜歡哪種體育活動？

820 What is your favorite book?
你最喜歡的書是什麼？

821 Which sport do you like the best?
那種運動你最喜歡？

822 What's your favorite music?
你最喜歡的音樂是什麼？

823 What type of music is your favorite?
那一種音樂是你最喜歡的？

824 What do you like to read?
你喜歡看什麼書？

825 Which newspaper do you read?
你看哪種報紙？

326 Which part of the paper do you read first?
你會先看報紙的哪一部分？

Answer
·應徵者回答·

327 I'm not much of a sports fan.
我不太怎麼迷運動。

328 I used to like baseball but I haven't played the game for five years.
我以前喜歡打棒球，不過有五年沒有玩了。

329 I have many hobbies.
I like almost all kinds of sports and I also like to listen to classical music.
我有很多愛好。
喜歡各種運動，也喜歡聽古典音樂。

830 I like playing basketball, and I also enjoy the team spirit of basketball.
我喜歡籃球及籃球活動中的群體精神。

831 During the weekend I often take the family out on short trips.
我常在週末帶著家人去旅行。

832 I like to travel on holiday
我喜歡在假期去旅行。

833 I like to spend the day in the countryside.
我喜歡去郊外活動活動。

834 I enjoy outdoor sports.
我喜歡戶外運動

835 I like to go on picnics or camping.
我喜歡去野餐和露營。

836 I like to play baseball, tennis and badminton.
我喜歡打棒球、網球和羽毛球。

837 Fishing is my favorite hobby.
釣魚是我的最愛嗜好。

838 My hobbies are hiking, fishing and climbing mountain.
我的嗜好是遠足、釣魚和爬山。

839 I like gardening and I have two dogs, which keep me pretty busy.
我喜歡園藝，我還養了兩隻狗，牠們已經把我忙得團團轉了。

840 I like almost all kinds of sports and listen to popular songs.
我幾乎喜愛所有的運動和聽流行音樂。

841 I read or go swimming.
If I have time, I enjoy camping in the wild with my friends.
我喜歡閱讀、游泳。
若時間許可，我愛和朋友到野外露營。

842 I like to listen to the music and to play piano and occasionally to go swimming and fishing.
我喜歡聽音樂、彈鋼琴，有時候去游泳和釣魚。

843 Flower arrangement is my favorite hobby.
插花是我最喜歡的嗜好。

844 I do a lot of reading and I enjoy it.
大部份的時間都在看書，我很喜歡看書。

845 I like reading the works of Jason L. Washington.
我喜歡讀傑森‧華盛頓的作品。

846 I read everything, but I like ghosts stories best.
我都讀，但我最喜歡看鬼故事。

847 I like to go to movies and read good novels.
我喜歡看電影和看好的小說。

848 I like popular music and classical music.
我喜歡流行音樂還有古典音樂。

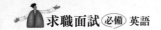

849 I guess calypso and Latin American music is my favorite.
我想黑人土風音樂和拉丁美洲音樂是我最喜歡的。

850 I also like to collect stamps, post cards, coins, and match boxes.
我也喜歡搜集郵票、明信片、錢幣和火柴盒。

851 My hobby is collecting antiques.
我的嗜好是收集古董。

Unit 16 面試結束

Question
•面試官提問•

852 Thank you very much for coming in to see us.
It has been a real pleasure talking with you.
謝謝你來見我們。
今天和你見面談得非常的愉快。

853 I have a reference from your present employer.
But I still have to interview four other candidates.
你現在的老闆已經給我推薦書了。
但我還得再面試其他四個應徵者。

854 Are you considering other job offers at this time?
你目前還有其他工作選擇嗎？

855 Thank you for coming for the interview.
I enjoyed talking with you.
謝謝你來面試。
我覺得我們談得很好。

856 Thank you for your time. Good-bye.
感謝你花費時間接受我的面試，再見。

857 Thank you, Mr. Brown, for your interest in this job. Good luck to you.
謝謝你對這份工作感興趣，伯朗先生，祝你好運。

858 I'll let you know in due time.
到時我會通知你的。

859 Thank you for coming.
We will let you know the result as soon as possible.
謝謝你的到來。
我們將儘早把結果通知你。

860 If we decide to hire you, we will notify you by mail.
如果我們決定雇用你，就寫信通知你。

861 If we decide to accept you, we'll notify you by E-mail.
假如我們要是決定用你的話，就用電子郵件通知你。

862 We should know by next Tuesday whom to hire. If your application is successful, we will notify you by mail.

下週二前我們會決定聘用誰。

若你申請成功，我們會發信函通知你。

863 I'll be writing to you in a few days. Thank you very much for your coming.

我過幾天就給你寫信。

謝謝你的光臨。

864 Leave your telephone number before you leave. We'll call you if anything comes up.

在你離開前請把電話號碼留下。

要是有任何消息我們就打電話給你。

865 We'll notify you next Monday at the latest. Shall I call you?

我們最遲下星期一就通知你。

我可以打電話給你嗎？

866 Thank you for coming in! We should know by next Wednesday whom we want to hire.

謝謝你來面試！

到下個星期三我們就應該知道我們要用那一位了。

867 I hope to see you again.
希望能再次見到你。

868 We'll expect you here next month. See you then.
我們期望下個月你的到來，再見。

869 Thank you very much for your advice. Bye.
非常感謝你的建議，再見。

870 You'll be hearing from us soon.
Send the next candidate in on your way out, please.
你很快會接到我們的消息。
出去的時候，請你叫下一位應徵人進來。

Answer
應徵者回答

871 Thank you for your time.
謝謝您撥冗接見。

872 Thank you for your time sir.
It was a pleasure speaking with you!
謝謝您的寶貴時間。
能夠和您談話是非常的榮幸。

873 A thousand thanks for your having talked with me. Good-bye.
非常感謝您的面試，再見。

874 Thank you, I'll look forward to hearing from you.
謝謝，我會恭候您的通知。

875 I'll await your notification.
Thank you for your interview with me, sir.
我將等候你們的通知。
謝謝您對我的面試，先生。

876 Thank you for your interview with me, Mr. White.
非常感謝您對我的面試，懷特先生。

877 Thank you, sir.
I hope to hear from you as soon as possible.
謝謝你，先生。
我希望盡快收到您的答覆。

878 When will I hear from you?
我什麼時候可以知道您的消息？

879 When can you give me your final decision?
您什麼時候可以給我你最後的決定？

880 Thank you very much. I'll be waiting for your letter.

多謝你，我就等著您的信好了。

881 I'll look forward to hearing from you. Thank you very much.

我恭候您的佳音好了。多謝！

882 Thank you for your consideration; then I will wait to hear from you.

謝謝關照，那麼我就等候您的消息吧！

883 Thank you, I will be expecting your call.

謝謝你，我就等候你的電話。

884 Do you have my number?

你知道我的電話號碼嗎？

885 You can contact me at my e-mail address, at (02)2345-6789, or 0953-123-456.

您可以寫email給我，也可以撥打(02)2345-6789 或0953-123-456與我聯繫。

886 I can be reached at 0953-123-456.

您可以撥打0953-123-456與我聯繫。

87 You can reach me at the above address or by phone at 0953-123-456.
您可以按以上地址或撥打 0953-123-456 與我聯繫。

88 I want to express my appreciation for giving me this chance.
I can assure you that you will not be disappointed.
能給我這個機會，我想表白一下我的感激。
我保證您，決不會失望的。

389 I feel confident that I would be able to do your job well, but do you have any doubts about my suitability?
我自信能做好這份工作，但請問在您看來我是否勝任？

890 I am confident you will find that my qualifications for this position merit your serious consideration.
我相信，您會認真考慮我的任職資格的。

891 I welcome an opportunity to discuss this position with you in more detail.
我希望能有機會和您更詳細地談談。

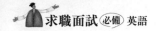

Unit 17 通過面試

Question
·面試官提問·

892 You are the very person we want.
你就是我們要的人選。

893 You are hired. When will you start to work?
你被綠取了。你什麼時候開始上班？

894 We will take you on.
If it is convenient for you, please come and work next Wednesday.
我們決定錄用你。
如果方便，請下週三來上班。

895 You are hired.
Please report to the personnel office April first at eight o'clock in the morning.
你已經被錄取了。
請你在四月一日早晨八點鐘到人事部報到。

896 Can you come this Wednesday with all your certificate and proof of work experience?
你可否在本週三來，帶來您的一切資格證書以及工作資歷證明？

97 If we decided to hire you, when could you start working?
假如我們決定錄用你的話，你什麼時候可以開始上班？

98 When will you be able to start to work?
你什麼時候可以開始上班？

899 When would it be convenient for you to begin work?
你什麼時候開始上班比較方便？

900 When would you be available to start work here?
你什麼時候可以開始來這邊上班？

901 When will you start to work?
你什麼時候可以開始上班？

902 How soon can you start? Could you tell?
你預計什麼時候可以來此工作？

903 You are employed. When will you start to work?
你被錄用，你什麼時候可上班？

904 Would you like to start work on Friday?
星期五就來上班如何？

905 Please come again next Monday morning, and I'll let you know what job we'll assign you.

請您下星期一上午再來，到時我會告訴您，我們給您指定什麼工作。

906 You'll be hired as a temporary employee first. In six months we will put you on our regular staff.

我們先以臨時雇員錄用你，六個月以後我們把你升為正式職員。

907 That's the way I like to hear young people talk. I think you'll make a valuable addition to our staff. When can you start?

我喜歡青年人這麼說話，我想你會成為一個很有用的員工，你什麼時候可以開始工作？

Answer
應徵者回答

908 Thank you for hiring me. I am very proud to be employed by your company.

謝謝你錄用我，承蒙貴公司錄用，本人至感驕傲。

909 I am available as soon as possible.

我隨時都可以上班。

10 I can start to work whenever it is convenient for you.

只要您方便，我隨時都可以開始工作。

11 I'll start to work tomorrow if you like.

您要是願意的話我明天就可以開始。

12 Thank you, sir. I will come in at eight o'clock sharp Monday morning.

謝謝你先生！我星期一早上準時八點到。

13 I can start anytime.

However, I'd like to give my present employer a day or two to find someone to replace me.

Is it alright if I start Monday?

我什麼時候開始都可以。

可是我想給我目前的老闆一或兩天的時間找一個人來替代我。

我星期一開始行不行？

14 I can't start tomorrow.

Because there is a few personal things I have to take care of.

Would Wednesday be alright?

我明天沒有辦法開始。

因為有一點私事我得處理一下。

星期三開始好不好？

915 I should consider a smooth transfer in my present post.
我得讓目前進行的工作平穩移交。

916 Could you please tell me what time allowance I would have to clear my desk?
你能給我多少時間讓我結束目前進行的工作？

917 If I am hired, I'll contribute whatever I can to bettering the after-sales service.
如果我被聘用的話，我將盡一切努力改善售後服務。

918 I'd like to serve on trial for a few weeks so that you can know for certain if I am appropriate for this job.
你們可以試用我幾週，看看我是否能勝任這個工作。

919 I know I am the right person for this job.
我知道我是最適合這個工作的人。

920 I'm afraid it doesn't fit me.
恐怕我是不合適 (這個工作)。

實用會話

光是懂得開口說英文還是不夠的，在面對英文面試時，你必須要將所學的【實用例句】融會貫通，才能顯現出你的英文實力。

本單元整理出面試時可能出現的狀況，加以模擬設計，提供了 34 種不同情境的【實用會話】，每一句都是簡單而實用的例句，讓你面對英文面試時，能夠見招拆招，再搭配【實用單字】的說明，讓你能夠徹底瞭解、運用在會話中。

除此之外，也建議您平時就要背誦與自己產業相關的英文專業用語，這可是您在尋找工作時，必備的專業技能，對於你的英文表達有相當大程度的幫助，應該平時就要多多加強這方面的實力。

Whatever is worth doing at all is
worth doing well.
凡是值得做的事情，都值得好
好地做。

Unit 1　電話通知面試

A : May I speak to Miss Jones?
我要找瓊斯小姐。

B : **Speaking**.
我就是。

A : This is Chris White the Personnel Manager of CNS. I've received your **application** and I'm very interested in your **qualifications**.
我是 CNS 公司人事部經理克里斯‧懷特，我已收到您的求職申請，我很感興趣。

B : I'm very glad to hear that.
聽到您這麼說，我非常高興。

A : I'm planning a meeting with you. I wonder if March 3 Wednesday morning at nine o'clock is ok with you.
我想給您安排面試。您看三月三日星期三上午九點怎麼樣？

B : March 3 Wednesday morning at nine o'clock......yes, that **suits** me.
三月三日星期三上午九點，對我來說很合適。

A: By that time, I'll be **expecting** you at my office. Do you know where our company is **located**?

到時，我會在辦公室等您。您知道本公司在什麼地方嗎？

B: I know it well, but I'm not sure how to find your office.

很清楚，但不清楚您的辦公室該怎麼找。

A: On the third floor of the first building, Room 392 with my name on the door.

在第一棟樓 3 樓 392 號房間，門上有我的名字。

B: I've got it. Thank you, Mr. White. I'll be **looking forward to** seeing you at your office on next Wednesday at nine o'clock.

清楚了。謝謝您，懷特先生，那我在下週三上午九點到您的辦公室來面試。

A: By the way, don't forget to bring your resume with you.

順便一提，別忘了帶你的履歷來。

B: I will.

我會的。

A: I will be expecting for you.

我會期待你的光臨。

關鍵單字　★　★　★　★　★　★

speaking	我就是 (適用於接電話者就是來電者要找的人時使用)
application	要求、請求、志願、申請、申請表格、申請書
qualification	資格
suit	合適、適宜、適合
expect	預期、預料、盼望、期待
locate	位於、在…地點
look forward to	預期、預料、期待、(喜滋滋地)盼望

Unit 2 安排面試時間

A: Good morning, this is IBM Company. How may I help you?
早安,這是 IBM 公司。有什麼需要我為您效勞的嗎?

B: Hello, may I speak to Mr. Smith, please?
您好,請找史密斯先生聽電話。

A: Wait a moment, please.
請稍候。

(稍後史密斯先生來接電話)

C: Jeff Smith speaking.
我就是傑夫・史密斯。

B: Good morning, Mr. Smith. This is Carol Ben, an **applicant** for the editor position.
您好,史密斯先生。我是卡羅・班,我向貴公司提出了編輯職位的申請。

C: Yes, and how can I help you?
是的,有什麼需要我幫忙的嗎?

B: Have you received my resume I sent out last Friday?
您收到我上星期五寄出的簡歷嗎?

C: Let's see..., yes, I have got resumes of two Carol Ben. Which Carol Ben are you?

我看看……是的，我收到了兩份名為卡羅・班的簡歷。您是哪個卡羅・班？

B: The one with a typing **certificate**. The telephone number I **indicated** is 4567-1234.

有打字證書的那個，我註明的聯繫電話是 4567-1234。

C: I see. I dialed the number a few minutes ago, but nobody answered the phone.

明白了。我幾分鐘前撥打這個號，但沒有人接電話。

B: I am sorry about that. I just came back from hospital.

那件事我很抱歉。我才剛從醫院回來。

C: It's ok.

沒關係。

B: I was wondering if you could **spare** me some time for an **interview** next week.

我想問一下，您是否可以在下星期替我安排個時間面試？

關鍵單字　★　★　★　★　★　★

applicant	志願者、請求者、申請者、應募者、候補者
certifica3te	證明書、許可證、執照
indicated	指示的
spare	節省使用、節約、不用、省卻
interview	會見、接見、會談、面試、面談

Unit 3　確認面試時間

A: I was just about to tell you about the **arrangement**. Can you be here next Monday?
我正想把面試安排通知您呢。您下星期一能來嗎？

B: Sure, at what time?
當然可以。什麼時間？

A: How about eleven o'clock?
十一點鐘如何？

B: Next Monday morning at ten o'clock. At your office?
下星期一上午十點鐘，在您辦公室嗎？

A: It's eleven o'clock, not ten.
是十一點鐘，不是十點。

B: Sorry, it's eleven o'clock.
對不起，是十一點鐘。

A: Yes, I will be expecting at my office.
是的，我會在辦公室等你。

B: I will be there on time.
我會準時到。

A: Do you know the **address** of our company?
你知道本公司的地址嗎？

B： Yes, I do.
　　是的,我知道。

A： And remember to bring your **autobiogrphy**.
　　還有,記得要帶你的自傳來。

B： I will.
　　我會(帶)的。

A： Thank you for your **interest**. See you next week.
　　謝謝您對本公司感興趣,下週見。

B： Good-bye.
　　再見。

關鍵單字　★ ★ ★ ★ ★ ★ ★

arrangement	協議、商定、約定、調解、和解、整頓、條理化
address	地址
autobiography	自傳
interest	興趣

Unit 4　正式面試前

A：May I help you?
有什麼需要我效勞的嗎？

B：I'm Sophia Brown coming for an interview. May I come in?
我是蘇菲亞‧布朗，來面試的。可以進來嗎？

A：Sure, come in please.
當然，請進。

B：Thanks.
謝謝。

A：Sit down **for a moment**, please. I will tell Mr. White you are here.
請稍坐，我會告訴懷特先生你來了。

（稍後）

A：Miss Brown, this way, please.
布朗小姐，這邊請。

B：Thank you.
謝謝。

（在懷特先生的辦公室）

A：Mr. White, **here comes** Miss Brown.
懷特先生，這是布朗小姐。

B：Hello, Mr. White.
懷特先生，您好。

A：Sit down please. I've been expecting you for a long time. Would you like coffee or tea?
請坐。我等你很久了。喝咖啡還是喝茶？

B：Tea, please.
茶就好。

A：**Here you are**.
請用。

B：Thank you.
謝謝。

● 關鍵單字 ★ ★ ★ ★ ★ ★ ★

for a moment	一會兒、一刻的功夫
here comes	某人來此、某人在此
here you are	給你、在這裡

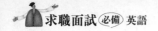

Unit
5　應徵原因

A: Good morning, Mr. Jackson. I am Sophia Parker.
早安，傑克森先生。我是蘇菲亞·派克。

B: Oh, come in, Miss Parker. Take this seat. I've been expecting you.
哦，派克小姐，請進。坐這兒。我正等您。

A: Thank you.
謝謝。

B: Do you know what made me **decide** to meet you?
您知道我為什麼決定面試您嗎？

A: No, I don't. What was it, please?
不知道。請問是什麼？

B: Your CPA certificate did. We think an **accountant** with a CPA certificate usually **performs** better than those **without**.
是您的註冊會計師證書。我們認為，獲得註冊會計師證書的會計，通常都比沒有獲得的做得出色。

A: Thank you for saying so. I think I am quite **competent** for the job.
謝謝您這麼説。我認為我能勝任這個工作。

B: Why did you choose this company?
您為什麼選擇了本公司。

A: I think this company is **expanding** rapidly and has a **promising future**.
我認為貴公司發展迅速，前景看好。

B: Yes, we are.
是的，我們的確是。

A: Besides, I know people here can **advance** on their **merits rather than** age.
此外，我知道貴公司員工是根據業績而不是根據年齡晉升的。

B: That's true. You really realize BBC.
那倒不假。你真的很了解 BBC。

A: That's what I want the most.
那是我最期盼的。

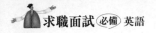

關鍵單字　　★ ★ ★ ★ ★ ★ ★

decide	決定
accountant	會計員、會計師、主計官
perform	做、進行、施行、執行 (任務)、履行(諾言等)、完成、 演(戲)、扮演(角色)、演奏、 彈奏
without	無、缺、沒有
competent	有能力的、勝任的
expand	擴大、膨脹、發展、增大
promising	有希望的、有前途的
future	未來的、將來的、今後的、 來世的
advance	升級
merit	價值、長處、優點、可取之處
rather than	寧願、與其…不如

Unit 6 自我介紹

Q: Tell me a little bit about yourself.
請介紹一下你自己。

A: My name is Peter and I live in Taipei, I was born in 1975. My major was sales marketing at Kasnsas State University.
我叫彼得，住在台北，出生於 1975 年。我在堪薩斯州立大學主修市場行銷。

Q: What kind of personality do you think you have?
你認為你有怎樣的性格？

A: I like developing fashion things and new ideas.
我喜歡流行事物和新點子。

Q: What would you say your **weaknesses** are?
你的弱點是什麼？

A: Well, I'm afraid I'm a poor speaker, however I'm fully **aware** of this, so I've been studying how to speak **in public**.
這個嘛……我不太擅長說話，我已經意識到這點，因此正在學習如何在公眾場所說話。

A: And **strengths**?
優點呢？

B: I suppose my strengths are I'm **persistent**, **optimistic** and a **fast-learner**.
我想我的優點是很執著、樂觀，而且學東西很快。

A: Do you have any **licenses**?
你有駕照嗎？

B: I have a driver's license.
我有駕駛執照。

A: How do you **relate** to others?
你和別人相處如何？

B: I'm very **cooperative** and have good teamwork spirit.
我非常能與人合作，富有團隊精神。

A: I see by your resume that you have been working?
從你的簡歷可以看出你一直在工作。

B: Yes, I have worked for two years with a Japanese Company.
是的，我一直在一家日本公司工作兩年。

6 關鍵單字 ★ ★ ★ ★ ★ ★ ★

weaknesses	弱點、缺點
aware	知道的、發覺的、意識到的、警惕的、警覺的
in public	公然、當眾
strength	強項、長處
persistent	堅持的、固執的、執意的、頑固的、持續的、繼續不斷的、不變的
optimistic	樂觀的
fast-learner	學習力快的人
license	許可證、證書、執照
relate	有關聯、使發生關係
cooperative	合作的、協力的、合作社的

181

Unit 7　在學成績

A: Do you bring your resume and your certificates with you?
你把簡歷和證書都帶來了嗎？

B: Here you are.
在這裡。

A: Good. Let me see.
很好。我看看。

(稍後看完履歷)

A: Would you tell me about yourself? Something like where did you go to school?
可以介紹一下你自己嗎？一些像是你在哪一所學校讀書？

B: I graduated from Michigan State University in last June.
我去年六月畢業於密西根州立大學。

A: What subject did you major in university?
你在大學主修的科目是什麼？

B: I majored in **economic** and **trade** English.
我主修的是商貿英文。

A: How were your **scores** in university?
你大學時的成績如何？

：They are above **average** 90. I have worked hard at my major subject.
我的平均成績在九十分以上。我對主修科目特別用功。

：What was your **favorite** subject at school?
在校時你最喜歡的科目是什麼？

：It's English writing.
是英文寫作。

：I can **judge** by your writing **skill simply** from your resume and application letter.
我可以從您的簡歷和附函看出您的寫作功力。

：Thank you for saying so. I enjoy writing.
謝謝你這麼説。我喜歡寫作。

關鍵單字 ★ ★ ★ ★ ★ ★ ★

economic	經濟
trade	貿易、商務
score	(考試、測驗的)分數、評分
average	平均的、一般、普通
favorite	偏好的、較喜愛的
judge	批評、指責、評論、判斷
skill	技巧
simply	簡單地、單純地

Unit 8　學歷簡介

A：Excuse me. May I see Mr. Chris Anderson, the manager?
抱歉，請問我能見經理克里斯・安德森先生嗎？

B：It's me. What can I do for you?
我就是。我能為你效勞嗎？

A：I have come to **apply** for the **position** as **secretary**.
我是來應徵秘書人員一職的。

B：OK. What's your name, please?
好的，請問你的名字？

A：My name is Sophia Loren.
我的名字是蘇菲亞・羅倫。

B：Please tell me what school you went?
請告訴我你的學歷好嗎？

A：I **graduated** from Michigan State University.
我畢業於密西根州立大學。

B：What are your **major** and **minor subjects**?
你的主修課和副修課都是些什麼？

A：My major subject is **Economics** and my minor subject is French.
我主修經濟學，副修是法語。

: What **courses** do you like best?
你最喜歡什麼課程？

: I **was very interested** in Business Management. And I think it's very useful for my present work.
我最喜歡企業管理，我覺得它對我現在的工作很有用處。

: When and where did you receive your **MBA degree**?
你的企管碩士學位是什麼時候，在哪裡授予的？

: I received my MBA degree from Michigan State University in 2002.
我於 2002 年在密西根州立大學獲得的企管碩士學位。

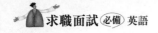
關鍵單字　★ ★ ★ ★ ★ ★ ★

apply	申請、請求、向某人要某物、查詢、詢問
position	職務、職位、位置、方位、地點
secretary	書記、秘書
graduate	大學畢業生
major	(為取得學位的)主修科目、主修
minor	(大學的)次要學科、選修課
subject	(講授的)學科、(考試的)科目、主題、問題、題目
Economics	經濟學
course	教程、課程、科目、單元
be very interested in	對某事非常有興趣
MBA	工商管理學碩士 (原文 Master of Business Administration)
degree	資格、地位、階級、身分、等級

Unit 9　學歷及工作經驗

: Good morning, Mr. Jackson.
傑克森先生，早安！

: Good morning, take a seat please. Would you **prefer** a tea or coffee?
早安，請坐。你想喝咖啡還是喝茶？

: **Neither**, thanks.
什麼也不要，謝謝。

: Do you bring the resume with you?
你有帶履歷嗎？

: Here you are.
在這裡。

（B 正在看 A 的履歷）

: I was **taken in** by your good resume, it looked **professional**. You are Comp-Specialty major, right?
我被你的這份好簡歷給吸引住了，寫得很專業。你的專業是電腦，對嗎？

: Yes, I'm the graduate of Taiwan university the year, here is my credit certificate and professor's **recommendation**.
是的，我是台灣大學的應屆畢業生，這是我的學分證明和教授的推薦信。

B: Do you have any working experience?
你有任何工作經驗嗎？

A: I have had a summer job for a **hardware** company. This is my employer's recommendation.
我在暑期曾經在一家硬體公司工作。這是我雇主的推薦信。

B: Good. Would you mind taking a test? It **consists of** two parts. Part one tests your EQ to **determine** whether your **personality** fits the job well. And part two tests your **skills background**.
很好。你願意參加筆試嗎？筆試由兩部分組成，第一部分是情緒智商測試，以確認你的性格是否適合這項工作。第二個部分則是專業背景測試。

A: I would love to.
我非常願意（參加測試）。

關鍵單字

★ ★ ★ ★ ★ ★ ★ ★

prefer	更喜歡、寧願選擇
neither	(兩者)都不的、兩者都不
take in	理解
professional	(需專門知識的)職業的、職業上的
recommendation	推薦、推舉
hardware	(電腦、計算機等)硬體設備
consist of	(由不同部分、要素)組成、構成
determine	決定、下決心(做某事)
personality	(明顯表現出來的)人格、個性、品性、性格、人品、魅力
skill	技巧、技術
background	背景

1 實用例句

2 實用會話

3 人事廣告

4 履歷表及自傳

Unit 10　筆試結果

A：I finished it.
我完成了。

B：You are **excellent** from the test results.
從測試的結果來看，你非常不錯。

A：Thank you. Do you mean I get the job?
謝謝，您的意思是說我得到這份工作了？

B：Before I give you a **definite** answer, I'll
consult with the **manage**ment and the
personnel department.
在給你肯定的答覆之前，我要和經理們以及人事
部商量一下。

A：I see. When can I expect an answer from you?
我明白了，我什麼時候可以得到答覆？

B：In two weeks.
兩週左右。

A：I would **appreciate** the opportunity to
discuss my qualifications with you in greater detail.
我希望能有機會跟您更加詳細地談談我的情況。

B: We'll **notify** you next Monday at the latest. Shall I call you?

我們最遲下星期一就通知你。我打電話給你行嗎？

A: Sure. You can contact me at my e-mail address sophia@yahoo.com, or call me at 0953-123-456.

您可以發電子郵件給我，是 sophia@yahoo.com 也可以撥打 0953-123-456 與我聯繫。

B: Thank you for coming. We will let you know the result as soon as possible.

謝謝你的到來，我們將盡早把結果通知你。

A: I will be waiting for your calls.

我會靜待你的來電。

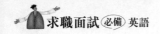
關鍵單字　★　★　★　★　★　★

excellent	極佳的
definite	界限明確的、範圍限定的、一定的、明確的
consult	商量、顧問
management	處理、控制、操縱、運用、經營、管理人員、經營者、管理部門、資方
appreciate	感激的、受歡迎的
notify	(正式)通知、通報、報告

Unit 11 專業能力

A: Would you tell me about yourself? Something like where did you go to school?
可以介紹一下你自己嗎？一些像是你在哪一所學校讀書？

B: Now I am a **graduate** student at Taiwan University studying **International Trade**.
現在我仍然在台大，在國際貿易系讀研究所。

A: Do you think you are **over-qualified**, then?
那你認為你資歷過高嗎？

B: I don't think it is a problem.
我不覺得那是個問題。

A: Did you get any **honors** or **rewards** at your university?
你讀大學時有沒有獲得過什麼榮譽或獎勵？

B: I got the university **scholarship** in 1998~2001 **academic** year.
我在 1998 到 2001 學年度獲得了學校獎學金。

A: You don't seem to have any experience in secretaries, do you?
你好像沒有任何秘書經驗，對嗎？

B : Although I have no experience in this field, I'm willing to learn about it.
雖然這方面我沒有經驗，但是我願意學習。

A : Would you tell me the **essential** qualities a secretary should maintain?
你能告訴我，作為一個秘書須具備什麼樣的重要素質？

B : I would say she needs to be **diligent**, and the second point is that she has to do a lot of things on her own initiative. Finally, she can make **report-writing**, **summary writing**, keep minutes at meetings, and so on.
我會認為她必須勤奮。第二，她必須主動做許多事情。最後，她應具有書寫報告、提要以及控制和作會議記錄的能力等等。

A : Absolutely. And most important of all is that she seems to have a better **memory** than average.
沒錯，而且其中，最重要的是比常人更強的記憶力。

B : That's truth.
這是事實。

● 關鍵單字 ★ ★ ★ ★ ★ ★ ★

實用例句 ①
實用會話 ②
人事廣告 ③
履歷表及自傳 ④

graduate	接受畢業文憑[學士學位]、得學士學位、畢業、獲得資格
International Trade	國際貿易
over-qualified	資格太高的
honor	榮譽、光榮、名譽、面子、體面、節操、尊敬、敬意、正義感、道義、自尊
reward	報酬、酬勞、獎賞、報答、報應、懲罰、(對歸還失物者、捕獲罪犯者)的賞金
scholarship	獎學金、獎學基金、獎學金制度、領取獎學金的資格
academic	學院的
essential	極其重要的、不可或缺的、絕對必要的
diligent	勤勉的、勤奮的、努力的、盡全力的、仔細的
report-writing	撰寫報告的能力
summary writing	下結論的撰寫能力
memory	記憶內容、記憶中的人[事]、留在記憶中的印象

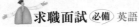

Unit 12　專業認證

A : Have a seat, please.
請坐。

B : Thank you.
謝謝。

A : So tell me why you **choose** the job we offer?
你為什麼選擇我們提供的這份工作？

B : My major at the university is just in line with the business **scopes** your company **deals** in.
我大學所學專業與貴公司所提的業務範圍相吻合。

A : What **additional training** and **schooling** have you had?
您還上過其他的什麼學校或受過其他的什麼培訓？

B : I got a teacher's certificate two years ago.
我兩年前取得教師資格證書。

A : What kind of part-time experience do you have?
你有什麼打工經驗？

B : I have worked at a **foreign representative** office in Seattle as an **intern** during my summer vacation.
我在暑假期間曾在一家外國公司西雅圖辦事處實習過。

A : How long have you been working there?
你在那兒工作多久了？

B : It's almost 3 months.
快要三個月了。

A : What have you been doing since you graduate from university?
大學畢業後你都在從事什麼工作？

B : I worked as a **field salesperson** for such companies as CNS, BCQ for three years. I learned a lot from the experience. I **gained** some **communication** skills in English.
我曾為 CNS、BCQ 等公司做過三年售貨員，學到了許多東西，培養了英文溝通能力。

A : What positions have you held at BCQ ?
你在 BCQ 擔任過什麼職務？

B : I was a Business Manager.
我是業務經理。

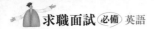

關鍵單字　★ ★ ★ ★ ★ ★ ★

choose	選擇
scope	(智力、研究、活動等的)範圍、領域、視野
deal	提及(問題等)、(與人)打交道、對待
additional	附加的、追加的、補充的、特別的
training	訓練、培養、練習、鍛鍊、教育、調教
schooling	學校教育、(函授教育的)課堂授課
foreign	外國的、外籍的
representative	代理人、代辦人、代表
intern	實習教師、實習生
field	(學問的)領域、範圍
salesperson	售貨員、店員、營業員
gain	得到、獲致
communication	聯絡、交通、傳達、傳播、訊息、口信

Unit 13 英語能力

A: Do you think you are **proficient enough** in both **spoken** and **written** English?

您的書面和口語英語應付得過來嗎？

B: My **former** employer was an American company, and most of my **superiors** were **native** English speakers. English is the working language there.

我以前任職的公司是一家美國公司，大多數上司的母語都是英語，英語是我們工作時所使用的語言。

A: What qualifications have you got?

你有什麼資格證書嗎？

B: Here are **reports** of the GMAT and TSE scores.

這是我的 GMAT 和 TSE 成績單。

A: Why did you take GMAT and TSE?

您為什麼參加 GMAT 和 TSE 考試呢？

B: To improve my English proficiency. In fact, I think taking examinations is an **efficient** way to learn a foreign language.

是為了提高英語水平。事實上我認為透過參加考試學習外語是一條有效的途徑。

A: GMAT and TSE are very **difficult**.

GMAT 和 TSE 非常難。

B: Yes, they are. To **prepare** for TSE, I took every possible **opportunity** to talk with native speakers.

是的，他們是很難。為了準備 TSE，我利用一切可能的機會和以英語為母語的人們交談。

A: You know our works are mostly **computerized**. Do you think you can **cope** with them?

我們的工作多數是用電腦操作管理的。你能勝任嗎？

B: I am very **skillful** at computer operating and using **programs** such as Office, AutoCAD, SPSS and so on. I am also good at writing programs in C language.

我能熟練地操作電腦，熟練地使用諸如 Office、AutoCAD、SPSS 等的程序，還擅長用 C 語言編程。

● 關鍵單字 ★ ★ ★ ★ ★ ★ ★

proficient	能手、專家
enough	有能力的、能勝任的、足夠的
spoken	口頭的、口說的、口語的
written	寫下的、文字的、書面的、成文的
former	從前的、先前的、以前的、(兩者中)前者(的)
superior	主管、上司
native	當地人的、天賦的
report	(調查、研究後提出的)報告(書)
efficient	功率[效率]的、有效的
difficult	困難的、艱難的
prepare	準備、預備
opportunity	機會
computerize	用電腦處理、用電腦檢索(情報)、使電腦化
cope	與…周旋
skillful	有技巧的、有技術的
program	程式

1 實用例句

2 實用會話

3 人事廣告

4 履歷表及自傳

Unit 14 英語溝通

Ⓐ：What are you interested in **besides** work?
除工作外，你還對什麼感興趣？

Ⓑ：Many things such as listening to the music, swimming, and traveling. I've been to many places.
我的愛好有許多，如聽音樂、游泳和旅遊。我去過許多地方。

Ⓐ：Which country have you ever been?
你去過哪一個國家？

Ⓑ：I've been to America three years ago.
我三年前去過美國。

Ⓐ：Really? I come from America. How do you think of her?
真的？我來自美國，你覺得美國是一個怎樣的國家？

Ⓑ：She is a free country.
她是一個自由的國家。

Ⓐ：Yes, she is.
是啊，她是。

Ⓑ：And I am planning to **join** a **travel tour** of America next year.
而且我計劃明年參加去美國的旅遊團。

A: Sounds interesting. Ok, tell me how much you know about this job we offer?

聽起來很有趣。好了,告訴我,你對我們的工作了解有多少?

B: The position you advertised **frequently involves** communication with native English speakers.

你們廣告招聘的這個職位,經常要與英語是母語的人士交流。

A: It's true.

這倒不假。

B: You can judge my spoken English by this meeting.

從我們的這次面談,您可以了解我的英語口語表達能力。

A: And this position is very **challenging**; and it **requires extra** work sometimes.

而且該職位也是非常具有挑戰性的,有時要加班。

B: Extra work is very common at my last company. I'm efficiency-oriented, so I'll try to **finish** my work **during** the **work hours**.

加班在我上一份公司是司空見慣的事。我是講求效率的,會盡量爭取在上班時間內把工作做完。

● 關鍵單字　★ ★ ★ ★ ★ ★ ★

besides	此外、另外、又…
join	參加、加入
travel tour	旅遊團
frequently	經常性地
involve	涉入、牽涉
challenging	挑戰性的
require	命令、要求
extra	額外
finish	完成、達成、達到
during	在…期間內
work hours	工作時間

Unit 15 工作目標

A: How do you know we need a reporter?
你怎麼知道我們需要一名記者？

B: I learned about it from your advertisement in the **newspaper**.
我是從報紙上你們的廣告中獲知的。

A: What interest you most about this job?
你對這份工作最感興趣的是什麼？

B: I think my major is **suitable** for this position.
我認為我的專業適合這個職位。

A: What do you think you would bring to the job?
你認為你將能為這份工作帶來什麼？

B: I am a very good team player and have the **desire** to make a **thorough success**.
我是一個很好的團體工作者，並有把工作做到最好的信念。

A: Do you choose this company on **account** of high pay?
你是因為薪水高才選擇本公司的嗎？

B：No, it's not. It's because I'm very interested in your company's training program.
不是的，是因為我對你們公司的培訓計畫很感興趣。

A：What do you **consider** important when looking for a job?
你選擇工作時主要的考慮是什麼？

B：I think the most important thing is the nature of the job. One should never do anything one is not interested in.
我認為工作的性質最重要，一個人千萬不要做沒有興趣的工作。

A：What's your **career objective**?
你的事業目標是什麼？

B：I would like to get a more **specialized** job.
我想獲得一份更加專業化的工作。

A：Why did you leave your former company?
為什麼離開以前的公司？

B：Because I want to change my working **environment**. I'd like to find a job which is more **challenging**.
因為我想改變工作環境，找一個更富有挑戰性的工作。

● 關鍵單字 ★ ★ ★ ★ ★ ★ ★

newspaper	報紙
suitable	適合的、適當的
desire	慾望
thorough	十分的、完全的
success	成功、成就
account	計算、帳單、結算帳單
consider	考慮、細想、思考、看作、認為
career	經歷、生涯、謀生之道、職業、成功、發跡
objective	目標、目的(物)
specialize	專門研究、專攻、詳細說明
environment	(有關生態、社會、文化方面的)環境、周圍的狀況
challenging	具挑戰性的、考驗能力的、引起爭論的

Unit 16 工作經驗 (一)

A: What is your working experience?
你的工作經歷是什麼？

B: I have worked for IBM.
我曾在 IBM 工作。

A: How will your experiences **benefit** this company?
你的經歷對公司有什麼好處？

B: I know the marketing from top to bottom and I can develop a new market for you. That will **increase** your profit **margin** and keep the **shareholders satisfied**.
我是對市場行銷非常熟悉。我能為貴公司開發新的市場，這會增加貴公司的利潤，讓股東們感到滿意。

A: What made you decide to change your job?
你為什麼決定換工作？

B: I would like to get a job in which I can **further** develop my career.
我想找一個工作進一步發展自己的事業。

A: May I ask you why you left the former company?
可以問一下你為什麼離開以前的公司？

B：Because I want to change my working
environment and seek new challenges.
因為我想換一下工作環境，迎接新的挑戰。

A：How long did you work there？
你在那裡工作多久？

B：I have been there for 4 years.
我在哪裡工作四年了。

A：How do you feel about your former
employer?
您覺得前一個雇主如何？

B：He is great. He knows how to manage a
company very well.
他知道該如何去管理一家公司。

A：How many places have you worked
altogether?
你一共工作了幾個地方？

B：Let's see..., CAW, POE, WTO, and IBM, it's
three.
我想想，CAW、POE、WTO 還有 IBM，總共三
個。

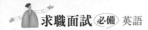
關鍵單字　★　★　★　★　★　★

benefit	益處、利潤
increase	增加、增大、增進
margin	(成本與售價的)差額、利潤、盈利、崗位[職務]津貼、補助費
shareholder	股票持有人、股東
satisfied	滿意的
further	更遠的、較遠的、更進一步的、深一層的、另外的、更多的 (far的比較級)
altogether	完全、全然、全部地、總共、總計、總起來說、總之、概括地說

Unit 17 工作經驗(二)

A: So tell me what made you decide to join our company?
所以,告訴我,你為什麼要加入敝公司?

B: What I really want is the chance to learn some advanced methods of management from foreign staff members.
我真正希望的是要從外國職員那裡學到一些先進的管理方法。

A: Why do you feel you will be **successful** in this work?
你為什麼覺得你能勝任這份工作?

B: I know I am the right person for this job. Besides, I think that my technical background is helpful for you.
我知道我是最適合這個工作的人。此外,我覺得我的技術背景對你們有用。

A: I can see that from your experience.
我可以從你的經驗裡看得出來。

B: I've done it so many time that I could do it blindfolded.
我不知做了多少遍了,現在蒙上眼睛也能做得好。

A: How would you **describe** you **accomplishments** in your last job?
在前一份工作中，您取得了什麼成就？

B: I could manage product **lifecycles**, provide training **sessions** on our products. This position need to **keep up** with the latest technology and trend.
我能管理產品銷售流程、準備和我們產品相關的培訓會議。這個職位必須能跟上最新的科技資訊及潮流。

A: What experiences have given you most satisfaction?
您取得的什麼經驗最令您滿意？

B: I have the ability to plan thoroughly and to **implement** effectively, the two traits of which are not often found in the same person.
我具備計劃及執行的能力，這兩點都具備的人不多。

A: Thank you for coming for the interview. I enjoyed talking with you.
謝謝你來面試，我覺得我們談得很好。

B: I am glad to hear that. I know I am the right person for this job.
我很高興聽見你這麼説。我知道我是最適合這個工作的人。

Ⓐ: That's right. You are the very person we want When can you start to work?
沒錯，你就是我們要的人選。你什麼時候可以上班？

Ⓑ: I must go back to Taipei to hand over my work and to go through necessary **procedures**.
我要回台北一趟，移交我的工作，辦理必要的手續。

關鍵單字　　★ ★ ★ ★ ★ ★ ★

successful	成功的、有成就的
describe	敘述、描寫、形容、說明、把(人)稱為…
accomplishment	實現、完成、成就、(出色的)成績
lifecycle	生命週期
session	(某項活動的)時期、(尤指)艱苦時期
keep up	支持、維持、使保持良好狀態
implement	使(協定等)生效[履行]、實行、滿足、達到
procedure	(行動、狀態、事情等的)進行、程序、手續、步驟

Unit
18 | 樂在工作

A: Why do you think I should **hire** you?
你為什麼認為我應該雇用你？

B: I believe my experience in **taxation** as well as my **familiarity** with the local business community would **enable** me to **contribute** to your **firm's** needs.
我熟悉本地商務情況，又有稅收方面的經歷，能夠為貴公司做出貢獻。

A: Would you mind working on **weekends**?
週末加班你會介意嗎？

B: I like it if it doesn't happen every day.
只要不是每天的話，我還是喜歡加班的。

A: What ideas do you have if we **employ** you?
如果我們錄用你，你有什麼想法？

B: I will **develop** my **potential** better while at the same time making my **contribution** to this company.
我能更好地開發自我潛能，為公司作貢獻的。

A: I am glad to hear that.
我很高興聽你這麼說。

B: I enjoy working hard.
對於努力工作我樂在其中。

A: I have a **reference** from your present
employer. But I still have to interview two other
candidates.
我已經從你現在的老板那裡拿到了推薦書。但我
還得再面試其他兩位應徵者。

B: I understand that.
我瞭解。

A: I enjoyed talking with you.
我們相談甚歡。

B: Thank you, sir. I hope to hear from you sooner.
謝謝你，先生。我希望盡快收到您的答覆。

A: Thank you for coming. We will let you know the
result as soon as possible.
謝謝你的到來，我們將盡早把結果通知你。

B: Thank you for your time. Good-bye.
感謝你花費時間接受我的面試，再見。

關鍵單字　★ ★ ★ ★ ★ ★ ★

hire	僱用、受雇
taxation	稅收、稅款
familiarity	通曉、精通、熟悉
enable	給(某人等)機會、使實現、使有效
contribute	獻出(主意等)、捐獻、捐贈(款項、藏書、食物、衣服等)
firm	(合夥經營的)商號、商行、(泛指)公司、企業
weekend	週末
employ	僱用
develop	進展、發育、發達、發展
potential	潛力
contribution	貢獻
reference	(身分、能力等的)證明書、介紹信、介紹人、證明人
candidate	候選人

Unit 19 薪資福利

: By the way, do you know anything about our salary system?
順便問一下,您知道我們的工資情況嗎?

: I **realize** that you **pay** higher than most foreign-owned companies in this city.
我瞭解貴公司比本市的多數外商企業工資要高些。

: As a general practice, the **starting** salary **ranges** from 30,000 to 35,000 a month.
一般說來,起薪每月在三萬元至三萬五仟元之間。

: How about the opportunities for **advancement**?
有無升遷機會?

: **Depending upon** your performance, **raises** may be offered after a **trial use** of three months.
經過三個月的試用後,依據表現,還會加薪。

: How about the benefits?
有沒有什麼福利?

: You can also enjoy **fringe benefits**.
另外還有些福利。

B: Could you give me a full detail of it?
能不能詳細說？

A: Such as monthly **bonus**, 10 day's **paid vacation** a year, and **health insurance**.
例如每月獎金、每年十天照發薪資的年假和健康保險。

B: That sounds OK to me. When can I know your final decision?
聽起來不錯。我什麼時候能知道您最終的決定？

A: I'll reach a decision before March 10. How can I contact you?
我會在三月十日前決定。我該怎麼與您聯繫？

B: You can reach me at 4568-0125.
您可以撥打 4568-0125 與我聯繫。

A: Thank you for your interest in this company. It's a pleasure talking with you. Good-bye.
謝謝您對本公司感興趣。和您交談真愉快，再見。

B: Good-bye.
再見。

關鍵單字　★ ★ ★ ★ ★ ★ ★

realize	明瞭、理解
pay	支付、付出
starting	開始的、起初的
range	區域、範圍
advancement	前進、進展、進步、發達、增進、促進、助長
depending upon	依據…
raise	提昇、增加
trial use	試用的
fringe benefits	附加福利
bonus	紅利、額外獎金
paid vacation	支付薪資的假期
health insurance	健康保險

Unit 20 提供推薦書

A: Can you **furnish** a letter of recommendation from CNS or BCQ?

能請 CNS 或 BCQ 公司提供一份你的推薦書嗎？

B: Of course.

當然可以。

A: Have you thought of **pursuing** a master's degree or something?

您是否想過攻讀碩士學位？

B: Yes, I used to consider obtaining EMBA degree.

是的，我曾考慮攻讀高階企管碩士學位。

A: Why didn't you do it?

您為什麼沒有這麼做？

B: I think I can **achieve** more academic progress if I have full time experience of two or three years.

我覺得，等有了兩三年的工作經驗再讀，效果會更好些。

A: That means you can't stay with us long if you are hired, right?

那就是說，如果我們聘用了您的話，您也不可能長期在這裡工作，對嗎？

B: Not exactly. If I am fortunate enough to be employed, I'll stay with you as long as I can be an asset to the company and at the same time **advance** my career **goal**.

不完全對。如果我有幸被聘用的話，只要我對公司有用，又能在事業上有所長進。我就會留在貴公司。

: We do **provide** numbers of opportunities to our employees.

本公司確實為員工提供了很多機會。

: How are employees **evaluated** and **promoted**?

公司如何評價和提拔職員？

: The position you are seeking now has a good **probability** to be promoted to the management.

您現在應徵的這個職位，就很有可能被提升至管理層。

: What I really want is the chance to learn some advanced methods of management from foreign **staff members**.

我真正希望的是要從外國職員那裡學到一些先進的管理方法。

A：I like aggressive employees. They are more likely to make contribution to the company.

我喜歡有進取精神的人。這種人更有可能為公司做貢獻。

關鍵單字 ★ ★ ★ ★ ★ ★ ★

furnish	提供、給予、(為…)供應
pursue	進行、從事、追求(目的)、追、追趕
achieve	完成、實現、建立、博得、達到(目的)
advance	提升、使晉級、進步、發展、進展、促進、成長
goal	目的地、要去的地方、目標
provide	提供生計、贍養、扶養、預備、預防
evaluate	評價、估價、估…值、定…價
promote	提升、提拔、擢升
probability	可能性、或然性、可能有
staff	全部工作人員
member	(團體的)一分子、成員、委員、團員

Unit 21 工作薪資

A: We do expect you to work **overtime** when it's **necessary**.
必要時我們需要你能加班。

B: I am not afraid of hard work; in fact, I enjoy it.
我不怕工作艱辛，實際上，我喜歡艱苦的工作。

A: Is that **acceptable** to you?
所以你能接受嗎？

B: Of course , I accept it.
當然，我接受。

A: And raises are given after three months' **probation period according** to your performance.
三個月試用期後將根據你的工作表現加薪。

B: I see. I think it is **reasonable**.
我了解。我覺得這很合理。

A: Is this satisfactory?
你滿意這樣的安排嗎？

B: Yes, it is quite satisfactory. I accept it.
是的，我很滿意，我可以接受這一安排。

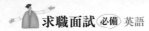
A: If you work all right after three months you will be put on the **permanent payroll** and be given a raise.

三個月試用後，如一切順利，將轉為正式員工並且加薪。

B: It's fine with me if I can be sure that there's a good chance to advance in this company.

假如我要是能夠在這個公司裏工作有升遷的機會的話，薪水好解決。

A: And we offer 2% **commission** on all your sales.

而且對你的銷售額我們將給予 2 % 的佣金。

B: When can I get the commission?

我什麼時候可以拿到佣金?

A: You'll get it at the end of each year.

每年年底你會得到佣金。

關鍵單字　★ ★ ★ ★ ★ ★ ★

overtime	超出規定的工作時間、額外工作
necessary	必要的、不可缺的、必然的、不可避免的
acceptable	可接受[受理、容忍]的、可忍受的
probation	驗證、檢定、見習(期)、實習(期)
period	一段時間、時期
according	根據…而定的、一致的、和諧的、相符的
reasonable	明白道理的、懂道理的、通情達理的、合理的、適當的
permanent	永久的、永恆的、不變的、耐久的
payroll	在職人員名單、薪水總額、在職人員總額
commission	手續費、傭金、回扣

Unit 22 薪資商議

A: What's the reason why you left your **previous** employer?
你離開原來那個雇主的原因是什麼？

B: The work is not bad. **Yet** the salary is too **small**.
那份工作倒是不錯，不過薪水太少了。

A: What were they paying you, if you don't mind my asking?
如你不介意我問這個問題，他們付你多少薪水？

B: I got 4,000 dollars per month.
我每個月薪資四仟元。

A: What are your salary expectations?
你對薪水有什麼期望？

B: I expect to be paid according to my abilities.
我希望能根據我的能力支付薪資。

A: So how much do you want?
所以你希望多少薪資？

B: With my experiences, I'd like to start at 6,000 dollars a month.
以我的經驗而言，我希望起薪是每月六仟元。

: Do you have any questions about us?
  你對我們公司有什麼問題嗎？

: I hope you'll consider my experience and training and will offer me a higher salary than the **junior** secretary's salary.
  我希望你們能考慮我的經驗及受過的培訓，給我定一份高於初級秘書的薪資。

: We will accept you for a three months' period of probation. And the salary is 5,500 per month. Do you mind about it?
  我們將先接受你三個月的試用期。而每月薪水是五仟五百元。對此你介意嗎？

: No, I don't mind being paid less than that. I **prefer** to learn more in a new position.
  不，我不介意，我寧願接受少一點的薪水而在新職位上多學一些東西。

關鍵單字　★　★　★　★　★　★

previous	先前的、以前的、早先的
yet	至今仍(未)、還、尚
small	小氣的、吝嗇的、卑鄙的、 小規模的、少的、些微的
ability	行事能力、能力
junior	資歷較淺的、地位較低的
prefer	更喜歡、寧願選擇

Unit 23 求職申請

A: May I know how many other companies you have **submitted** your application?
請問您向幾家公司提出了求職的申請？

B: None but yours. How many **candidates** do you have for this **opening**?
只有貴公司。請問該職位有多少候選人？

A: By now I've chosen only one for interview out of **dozens** of applicants.
迄今為止，我們從幾十個申請者中只選出了一個。

B: Thank you, sir.
謝謝您。

A: You are the first and maybe the last to be interviewed for this position.
您是我面試的第一個人，或許是最後一個吧。

B: I'll be honored if you offer me the job.
能得到這份工作的話，我將非常榮幸。

A: I am glad to hear that. How much do you make at your **current** job?
我很高興聽見你這麼說。你目前的工作薪資是多少？

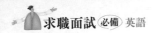
B : I'm presently making thirty thousand a
month.
我目前的薪水是三萬元。

A : How do you expect your salary?
您的希望工資是多少？

B : I don't know how much you pay for such work to
an average employee.
我不知道貴公司對這個職位一般給多少薪資？

A : We usually require three months of trial
employment. **During** this period we offer a monthly salary of 30,000.
對於新聘人員，我們通常要求試用三個月，這期
間的月薪是三萬元。

關鍵單字 ★ ★ ★ ★ ★ ★ ★

submit	提交、呈遞、提出(意見等)、委託、託付
candidate	候選人
opening	開幕、開場、開、開放、開始、開通
dozen	一打的、十二個的、(同樣東西的)(一)打、12個
current	(貨幣)流通的、(謠言)流傳的、(意見)流行的、現時的、當前的、眼下的、最新的
during	在整段時間、在整個時期

Unit
24　加薪福利

A : May I know when I would get a raise?
我想知道我何時可以加薪？

B : If you are found to be competent for the post, the monthly salary will be raised to 35,000, bonus or other compensations not included.
如果您能勝任本工作，月薪將提高到三萬五千元，不包括獎金和其他補貼。

A : Any other welfare packages for the first three months?
前三個月有沒有其他的什麼福利？

B : I am afraid not. But if you stay here after three months, you'll find our welfare packages are very satisfactory.
恐怕沒有。但如果三個月後被留用的話，福利待遇會很可觀。

A : How satisfactory?
有多可觀？

B : Maybe your bonus and other compensations will be half as much as your salary.
也許獎金和補貼可能有您薪資的一半多。

A : I think it's acceptable.
我覺得可以接受。

Unit 25 私人問題

A: What is the most important thing for you to be happy?
對你來說最重要的是什麼？

B: For me, this would be having good **relationship** with my family members.
對我來說，最重要的是保持和家人的良好關係。

A: Would you tell me something about your family?
請告訴我一些你家裡的事情。

B: My father is a Chinese teacher, and my mother is a **housekeeper**. Both my brother and sister are studying at school.
我父親是一名中文老師，而我母親則是一位家庭主婦。我的弟弟妹妹都還在學校上學。

A: Do you **spend** much time staying with your family?
你花很多時間與家人在一起嗎？

B: During the weekends or holidays, we sometimes go to parks, **cinemas**, and **concerts** together.
週末和假日期間，我們一家人有時會一起去公園、看電影、聽音樂會。

A：You may ask questions about us, if you have any.
如果有什麼問題，你可以提問。

B：Can you tell me a little about work time or employee benefits such as the health insurance program?
能告訴我關於工作時間或健康保險之類的員工福利嗎？

A：5 working days **per** week, 12 days of **annual** holiday per year, 14 months of salary is fixed, extra bonus can be expected.
每週週休二日、一年十二天假期、十四個月固定薪金，並另外有紅利。

B：It sounds perfect.
聽起來很棒！

A：What are your great strengths?
你有什麼優點？

B：I can work under **pressure** and **get along with** my **colleagues**.
我能在壓力下工作，並能與同事和諧相處。

A：In what specific ways will our company benefit from hiring you?
我公司僱用你有什麼好處？

B : I'm very familiar with this market and have many customers. I think your company will benefit from it.
我對這個市場非常熟悉並有許多客戶，我認為貴公司能從中獲益。

● 關鍵單字　　★ ★ ★ ★ ★ ★ ★

relationship	關係、關聯
housekeeper	家庭主婦
spend	用(錢)、花費、支出、花(時間)、度過、消磨
cinemas	電影院
concert	音樂會
per	每個、每…、每一
annual	一年的、年度的、年年的、一年一次的、全年的
pressure	壓力
get along with	和睦相處、相處得好、相處得好
colleague	同僚、同事

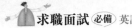

Unit
26 個人特質

A: What **section** would you like to work in if you **enter** this company?
如果你被本公司錄用，你希望在哪一個部門工作？

B: I'd rather work in the magazines department if **choices** may be given.
如果可以選擇，我願意在雜誌部門工作。

A: Do you have any **particular conditions** that you would like the company to take into consideration?
你有什麼特殊情況需要公司加以考慮嗎？

B: I can take on jobs that bother other people and work at them slowly until they get done.
我能承擔別人認為麻煩的工作，然後慢慢努力，直到把工作完成為止。

A: What are your **weak points**?
你的缺點是什麼？

B: I think I'm a bit shy around people. That is my weakness. But I'm very patient both with people and my work.
我覺得我在眾人面前有些害羞，這是我的缺點。但是我對人和對工作都非常有耐心。

A: What kind of people do you like to work with?
你最喜歡和哪類人合作？

B: I like to work with people who are **honest**, **dedicate** to their work and have **integrity**.
我喜歡和誠實、對工作投入、為人正直的人一起工作。

A: What are the problems you have **encountered** in your job?
你在工作中曾遇到過哪些困難？

B: I liked the work. However, my last firm is too small for me to **widen my** experience.
我喜歡那份工作。但前一家公司太小了，難以增加我的工作經驗。

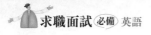

關鍵單字 ★ ★ ★ ★ ★ ★ ★

section	(政府機關、團體的較小部門) 處、科、股、組
enter	進入、入學
choice	選擇、挑選、選擇的自由、 選擇能力
particular	特殊的、特別的、特定的、 特指的
condition	狀態、狀況
weak	懦弱的、弱的
point	狀況、特點
honest	誠實的、正直的、公正的、 正派的
dedicate	把(時間、精力等)用於
integrity	(道德、人格的)正直、誠實、 高潔
encounter	遭遇、碰見
widen	(使)變寬、(使)變闊

Unit 27 接受工作

A: What do you know about our major products and our share of the market?

關於本公司的產品和市場分配額你知道些什麼？

B: Your company's products are mostly marketed in the United States, but particularly has sold very well here in Taiwan.

貴公司的產品主要在美國市場銷售，但是特別在台灣市場的銷路非常好。

A: Are you aware of the **aspects** of this position and do you feel you are qualified?

你對這個職位了解嗎？你認為自己資格符合嗎？

B: Yes, I understand my qualification and your needs by **researching** your company.

是的，透過對你們公司的研究，我理解你們的要求，並認為我能勝任這個職位。

A: If you enter this company, what section would you like to work in?

如果能進入公司，你想在哪個部門工作？

B：If possible, I'd like to be **positioned**
International Trade Department.
可能的話，我想在國際貿易部門工作。

A：What starting salary do you expect?
你想要多少起薪？

B：I'd like to start at 50,000 dollars a month.
我想要每月五萬元。

A：How long does it take to get here from your
home?
從你家到公司要花多少時間？

B：It takes about 30 minutes **ride**.
搭車大約 30 分鐘。

A：What else do you want to know?
你還需要知道其他的事嗎？

B：What are the company's working hours?
公司的上下班時間是怎樣的？

A：It's from nine to six, twelve to one is
lunchtime.
從九點到六點，中午十二點到一點是午餐時間。

關鍵單字 ★ ★ ★ ★ ★ ★ ★

aspect	形勢、狀況、局面、看法、解釋
research	(學術)研究、調查
position	職務、職位
ride	搭乘(馬車、汽車、公車等)

Unit 28　連絡方式

A：Do you have any further questions?
你還有其他進一步的問題嗎？

B：Yes, do you have **allowance** for
transportation as well as a housing packages,
medical insurance, **unemployment**
insurance and **annuity**?
是的，你們有交通補貼、醫療保險、失業保險及養老金嗎？

A：Yes, we have. And you'll also enjoy **life insurance**
and **health insurance**, a two-week paid vacation a
year.
是的，我們有，而且你將享受人壽保險和健康保險，一年一次為期兩週的帶薪假。

B：I see.
我瞭解。

A：It's an excellent benefits package.
那是很好的福利。

B：Would there be any opportunities to work
abroad in the future?
將來有機會到國外工作嗎？

A : I am afraid not. Why?
恐怕沒有。為什麼這麼問？

B : Beacues I don't want to work abroad.
因為我不想去國外工作。

A : How can I **contact** you when we reach our decision?
我們決定後如何跟你聯繫？

B : My **cellular phone** number is 0953-000-000.
我的手機是 0953-000-000。

A : Let me write it down.
我寫下來。

B : You can call me at this number between 2 and 6 in the afternoon.
你可以在下午二點到六點之間用這個號碼打電話給我。

A : Do you have any questions you would like to ask me?
您還有問題要問嗎？

B : That's all. Thank you for your time.
就這樣了。謝謝你撥冗面試。

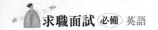

● 關鍵單字　★　★　★　★　★　★　★

allowance	(定量的)津貼、支給額、分配額
transportation	運費、交通費、旅費、運輸、運送、搬運
medical	醫療的、醫學的、醫用的
unemployment	失業(狀態)、失業人數[率]
annuity	年金、年紅利、年金享受權
life insurance	人壽保險
health insurance	健康保險
abroad	到國外、在國外
in the future	將來、今後
contact	聯絡、(相互)接觸、聯繫、建立聯繫
cellular phone	行動電話

Unit 29 獲得錄取

Ⓐ : What kind of people do you find difficult to work with?

你覺得和哪類人合作最困難？

Ⓑ : I think people who are not cooperative are not easy to work with.

我認為沒有合作精神的人是不容易共事的。

Ⓐ : What would be your **response** if we put you in Sales Department?

如果我們派你去行銷部工作你願意嗎？

Ⓑ : I think I am rather **outgoing**. I enjoy working with others.

我想我較外向，我喜歡和別人合作。

Ⓐ : It's not as easy as it seems.

它不像看上去那麼容易。

Ⓑ : I think I can, and I don't mind hard job.

我想我能做到，我不怕工作艱苦。

Ⓐ : New **employees** here often have a heavy **work-load**.

這兒的新雇員經常需要超負荷工作。

B: It's no problem for me. I believe I can do anything for you.
對我來說毫無問題，我相信我能為您做任何事情。

A: What would you like to be doing after three years about your job?
三年後你希望對自己的工作有何期望？

B: I hope to have a job; which offers me an opportunity for advancement.
我希望有一個提供升遷機會的工作。

A: I **promise** it to you that it is a permanent job with promotions and rises if you work hard.
我向你保證，這是一份固定的工作，將來能夠有升遷或者加薪的機會，只要你努力工作。

B: I always give each job my best **efforts**.
我做每份工作總是全力以赴。

A: I hope you will be happy working with our firm.
我希望你在我們公司裡工作愉快。

B: I won't let you down.
我不會讓您失望。

◯: How can we get **in touch with** you?
我們怎樣和你聯繫？

B: You can reach me at 6254-7833.
你可以打電話給我，號碼是 6254-7833。

關鍵單字 ★ ★ ★ ★ ★ ★ ★

response	回答、答覆
outgoing	好交際的、性格外向的
employee	受僱者、僱員、從業人員
workload	工作量
promise	諾言、承諾
effort	努力、奮鬥、勤勉、(募捐等的) 活動
in touch with	和…接觸、和…一致

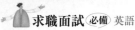

Unit 30 用電子郵件通知錄取

A: What starting salary would you expect here?
你期望在這裡起薪多少？

B: Since this will be my job and I don't have much experience, I feel **hesitate** to **suggest** salary.
由於這是我的工作，又缺乏工作經驗，所以不敢貿然提出待遇要求。

A: I see. Would you consider a starting salary at 40,000 dollars?
我了解。你可以考慮起薪每月四萬元嗎？

B: I'm quite satisfied with the salary. That would be more than I have expected.
我很滿意這個薪資，比我期望的要多。

A: Do you have any other questions?
你還有任何其他問題嗎？

B: When can I know whether I am accepted or not?
我什麼時候才能知道是否被錄用呢？

： We will let you know probably next week. I hope to give you the positive **reply**.

我們大概會在下星期讓您知道，我希望給你肯定的答覆。

： Thank you, I will be glad to hear that.

謝謝，如能聽到這消息我將很榮幸。

： By the way, have you got an e-mail account?

順便問一下，你有電子郵件信箱嗎？

： Yes, it's sophia@yahoo.com.

有的，是 sophia@yahoo.com。

： OK. Let me write it down.

好，讓我把它抄下。

（稍後）

： When will you let me know the result **at the latest**?

你最遲何時會通知我結果？

： We should know by next Tuesday whom to hire. If your application is successful, we will notify you by e-mail.

下週二前我們會決定聘用誰，若你的申請成功，我們會發電子郵件通知你。

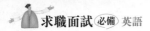
關鍵單字 ★ ★ ★ ★ ★ ★ ★

hesitate	躊躇、猶豫、遲疑不決、 有顧慮、不好意思
suggest	建議、提議、提出、暗示、 間接地表明、意指
positive	確實的、明確的、 無可懷疑的、很難否定的
reply	回答、答覆、反應、應答
at the latest	至遲、最晚至

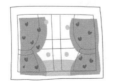

Unit 31 用電話通知錄取

: I think you'll find I'm **worth** it.
我想你會發現我是值得的。

: I am glad that you are so **confident**. When can you start to work here?
我很高興你如此自信。你何時可以到這裡上班？

: I can't start on this month. There are a few **personal** things I have to **take care** of.
這個月我不能上班，我有一些個人事務需要處理。

: When is it more convenient to you?
你何時較方便？

: I can start to work in a week.
一個星期後我可以開始工作。

: So it's 5th November, right?
所以是十一月五日？

: Yes, it's.
是的。

A: Good. By the way, how can I reach you?
很好。對了，順道一提，我如何與你聯絡？

B: You can reach me at 3657-8945.
你可以打電話給我，號碼是 3657-8945.

A: Is it 3-6-5-7-8-9-4-5?
是 3-6-5-7-8-9-4-5 嗎？

（重複念電話號碼以確定無誤）

B: Yes. In case I'm not there, please leave a message and I will call back for your **instruction**.
假如我不在，請留言，我將打回電話詢問您的指示。

A: If you are satisfied with the conditions here, please sign on this **contract**.
如果你對這裡的條件滿意，請在合約上簽名。

B: I really appreciate your **assistance**.
衷心感謝您的幫助。

● 關鍵單字　　　★ ★ ★ ★ ★ ★ ★

worth	價值、真正的價值、值得
confident	充滿自信的
personal	個人的、私人的、一身的、自身的、與個人有關的
take care	當心、注意設法、竭力
instruction	指示、說明、使用說明書
contract	契約、合約
assistance	幫助、幫忙、協助、援助、輔助

Unit 32 考慮接受工作

A: I want to **express** my **appreciation** for giving me this chance. I can **assure** you that you will not be disappointed.

您能給我這個機會，我想表白一下我衷心的感激。我保證你決不會失望的。

B: If we take you on, when you will be able to start to work?

如果我們決定錄用你，你什麼時候可以上班？

A: I didn't expect you would have accepted my application at the first interview.

我沒想到首次的面試，貴公司就接受了我的申請。

B: Do you need more time to **consider** our offer?

你需要多一點時間考慮我們的提議嗎？

A: Yes, I need some time to consider it.

是的，我需要多一點的時間考慮。

B: Sure. You have to let me know your **decision before** next Wednesday.

當然好，你必須在下週三前讓我知道你的決定。

A: Sure, I'll let you know my decision before May 20.

當然，我會在五月廿日前把最終的決定告訴您的。

B: I'll be expecting your reply. If you have any questions about the company or the post, please don't **hesitate** to let me know.

我等您的答覆。如果對本公司和該職位有什麼疑問的話，請儘管問我。

A: Thank you for your time and offer, Mr. Smith. Good-bye.

謝謝您的撥冗及協助，史密斯先生。再見。

B: Good-bye.

再見。

關鍵單字 ★ ★ ★ ★ ★ ★ ★

express	表達(感情等)
appreciation	感謝[承認、讚賞]的表示
assure	使確信、保證、擔保
consider	考慮、細想、思考
decision	決心、決意、決定、解決、決議、判決、結論
before	以前、以往、已經、較早(時間)
hesitate	延遲、延誤

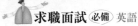

Unit 33 面試結束

A : We'll **notify** you next Friday at the latest. Shall I call you?
我們最遲下星期五就通知你。我打電話給你行嗎？

B : I will be waiting your phone call.
我會期待你的來電。

A : **Since** there are **other** applicants on the line, we can't let you know our decision yet until all of them have got their chance for interview.
因為還有其他應徵者，所以，直到所有有機會面試的人面試完畢後，我們才能將決定通知你。

B : Fair enough, I am willing to wait until you have **come to** a decision.
那很公平，我願意等候您下決定。

A : Good. I believe I will call you next week.
很好，我相信我下週會打電話給你。

B : I'll await your notification. Thank you for your interview with me, sir.
我將等候你們的通知，謝謝您對我的面試，先生。

A：Thank you for coming for the interview. I enjoyed talking with you.

謝謝你來面試，我覺得我們相談甚歡。

B：I want to express my appreciation for giving me this chance.

您能給我這個機會，我想表白一下我衷心的感激。

A：You earn this chance by yourself.

是你自己爭取這個機會的。

B：Thank you anyway.

還是謝謝您。

A：We'll expect you here next month. See you then.

我們期望下個月你的到來，再見。

B：Good-bye.

再見。

● 關鍵單字　　★ ★ ★ ★ ★ ★ ★

notify	(正式)通知、通報、報告
since	從那以後、從那時以來、後來
other	(兩個中)另一的、(三個以上中)剩下一個的、外的、其他的、別的
come to	達成協議

Unit 34 進入新公司

A: Good morning Mr. Smith. It's **pleasure** to meet you again.

早安,史密斯先生,我很榮幸再見到你。

B: Nice to see you, Miss Jones, if you work hard, sky's the **limits** here.

很高興見到你瓊斯小姐,好的開始是成功的一半。希望你前途無量。

A: Thanks. Shall I meet my colleagues?

謝謝,我能見見同事嗎?

B: Sure, come with me.

當然可以,跟我來。

(稍後 B 介紹 A 與同事 C 認識)

B: David, I would like you to meet our new **comer**, Sophia, she just graduated from Iowa State University.

大衛,我向你介紹一位新同事蘇菲雅,她剛剛從愛荷華州立大學畢業。

C: Nice to meet you.

很高興認識你。

A: Nice to meet you too. I am new to the working world and appreciate your guidance.
我也很高興認識你。我沒有什麼工作經驗，請您多指教。

B: That's all right. I will try my best to **assist** if you need any help.
別客氣，如果需要幫忙，我會盡力的。

A: Great! Thank you.
太好了。謝謝你。

B: Well, as other guys are still not in, I'll introduce you to them later.
其他人還沒來，我晚些時候介紹給你。

A: All right. Nice to meet you, David.
好吧。很高興認識你，大衛。

C: Me too. See you later.
我也是。待會見。

關鍵單字 ★ ★ ★ ★ ★ ★ ★

pleasure	愉快、快樂、滿足、歡愉、喜好、希望、
limit	限定、限制
comer	來者、已經來的人
assist	援助、幫助、輔助裝置

Part

3

人事廣告

人事招聘廣告是企業主與求職者之間的第一次接觸。如果你想要獲得一份滿意的工作，首先，你必須看得懂人事招聘廣告。

人事廣告的內容有別於一般生活或學習性閱讀，在閱讀的過程中，您必須具備一定的閱讀技巧及對應徵職務的基本認知，否則許多人事廣告對您而言，可能會猶如有字天書般令你摸不著頭緒，本書也提供許多職位的英文名稱供您參考（詳見第 305～314 頁），讓您取得事半功倍的效果。

在追求效率化的廿一世紀，企業主會利用有限的版面，刊登最有效的人事廣告，因此人事廣告往往會利用最簡潔的文字說明企業背景、招聘的職位。為了能從浩如瀚海的招聘廣告中迅速找到自己中意的職位，我們在閱讀時，須盡量用最少的時間讀到盡可能多的廣告，因此你必須利用最少的時間、最快的速度，徹底瞭解人事廣告所傳遞的關鍵訊息，包括職位、職責、資格、待遇、工作地點等，等到你確認自己所中意的人事職位時，就可以開始下一步自傳、簡歷的撰寫了。

諺 語

There is a time and a place for everything.

說話看場合，做事看時機。

人事招聘 ---○ 公司簡介 (一)

A five days working week with two holidays

週休二日

Medical insurance

醫療保險

Two-week vacation each year

兩週的年假

Fringe benefits

附加員工紅利

人事招聘 ---○ 公司簡介 (二)

We offer Competitive salary, Stock sharing,
Project bonus, and Moderate training, Certification
training...

本公司提供有競爭力的薪金、員工認股、專案紅
利、基本培訓、認證培訓……等。

1 實用例句

2 實用會話

3 人事廣告

4 履歷表及自傳

人-事-招-聘 ···∘ 公司簡介（三）

We offer an excellent compensation and benefits package including a 5-day week, medical scheme, purchase discounts, retirement program.

本公司提供良好的薪金及福利，包括週休二日、醫療規劃、員工購物優惠、退休計劃。

人-事-招-聘 ···∘ 公司簡介（四）

We offer attractive compensation package, excellent working environment. For the right people, our growing organization offers plenty of career opportunities.

本公司提供極具吸引力的競爭性薪金、良好的工作環境，對於合適的人選而言，我們日益成長的組織機構提供了大量就業機會。

人-事-招-聘 ···∘ 公司簡介（五）

5 days working per week, 10 days of annual holiday per year, 14 months of salary is fixed, extra bonus can be expected.

每週週休二日、一年十天假期、十四個月基本固定薪資，並另有紅利。

⊙**Director of Marketing and Sales Division**

The successful candidate should fulfill the following requirements:

5 years of working experience in Marketing/ Sales

University degree, preferably in technical science

Good English

Knowledge in Ms-Office Application

Outgoing personality

Interested candidates please send your detailed resume both in English and Chinese with contact phone, recent photo and expected salary to:

9F., No. 194-1, Sec. 3, Datong Rd., Sijhih Dist, New Taipei city 221, Taiwan (R. O. C.)

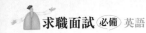
⊙行銷部門主管

應聘者須符合下列條件：

5 年市場／銷售相關工作經驗

大學畢業，科技相關學科畢業者尤佳

英語良好

熟悉 Ms-Office 軟體

個性外向

有興趣者可將中英文履歷表，註明聯絡電話、近照、希望待遇，郵寄至中華民國台灣新北市汐止區大同路三段 194 號 9 樓之一

人事招聘 ⸺ 外銷部經理

⊙ Export Sales Manager

Five years of related work experience in direct marketing

A master's degree in business administration

Strong interpersonal skills

Experience in leading a team

Fluency in English both speaking and writing

Also prefer to have German capability

⊙ 外銷部經理

5 年的直效行銷相關工作經驗

工商企業管理碩士

人際交流溝通能力強

具領導團隊部門的經驗

英文說寫流利

具備德語能力者尤佳

人-事-招-聘 ⋯⋯ 財務分析員

⊙ **Financial Analyst**

Above age 35, B.A. degree

Good communicator in English

Excellent command of financial situations

Job Descriptions:

Analyzed economic and financial situations

Audited financial transactions

Prepared variety of accounting reports

⊙ **財務分析員**

35 歲以上，學士學位

擅長以英文溝通者

具良好的財務分析能力

工作說明：

分析經濟和財務狀況

審計財務交易

製作各種會計報表

人-事-招-聘 ⊶⊶ 執行秘書

⊙**Executive Secretary**

Previous experience as top management executive

Can work independently and under pressure

Initiative and to facilitate top executive carry out major tasks

Fluency in English both speaking and writing

Also prefer to have Japanese capability

Certain experience in the administration function

University degree, preferably in journalism

⊙**執行秘書**

有高層管理執行經驗

能獨立作業並能承受工作壓力

有進取心，能協助高層主管執行主要任務

英文說寫流利

具備日文能力者尤佳

有一定行政經驗

大學畢業，傳播相關學科者尤佳

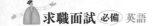
人·事·招·聘 ⸰⸰⸰ 倉儲經理

⊙ **Warehousing Manager**

Above age 40

6 years exp. in cosmetics/ pharmaceutical field

Independent, cost saving, clean concept

College graduate or above

Good English

Familiar with PC Windows

Located in Taipei

⊙ **倉儲經理**

40 歲以上

6 年化妝品／藥物領域相關經驗

能獨立作業、節約開銷、觀念明確

專科以上畢業

英文良好

熟練 PC 的 Windows 系統操作

工作地點在台北

人·事·招·聘 —○—○— 客服部主管

- ⊙**Customer Service Sup.**

  Management exp., customer service oriented

  Fluency in English both speaking and writing

  University degree

- ⊙**客服部主管**

  有管理經驗，以為顧客服務為導向

  英文說寫流利

  大學畢業

人·事·招·聘 —○—○— 廣告業務經理

- ⊙**Advertising Manager**

  Under age 35, male

  Good English, B.A. degree

  Can work independently and under pressure

  Major Responsibility:

  To sell advertising space in the Time magazines

  to clients and agencies

- ⊙**廣告業務經理**

  35 歲以下，男性

  英文良好，學士學位

  能獨立作業並能承受工作壓力

  主要工作職責：

  向客戶和代理商推銷《時代雜誌》的廣告欄

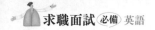

人・事・招・聘 ---◦◦ 採購經理

⊙ **Purchasing Manager**

University/college graduate or above, major in
Technical related fields

Mini 5 years of Purchasing/International
Trading experience

Good command of English in written &
speaking

Also prefer to have German capability

Willing to have oversea trips for Export oriented
business

Familiar with PC Windows Package

⊙ 採購經理

大學／大專以上學歷，主修科技相關領域

至少有 5 年採購或國際貿易經驗

英文說寫流利

具備德文能力者尤佳

願意為出口業務出國

熟練 PC 的 Windows 系統操作

人·事·招·聘  電話服務人員

⊙CSR Rep.

Job Descriptions:

Handle Customers' telephone inquiry regarding
Billing Statements, Marketing Promotions,
Financial Services and Product features.

⊙電話服務人員

工作職責：

處理顧客詢問有關賬單明細、促銷活動、財
務服務及產品特色等事宜。

人·事·招·聘 銷售助理

⊙Sales Assistant

Responsibilities:

Administration assistance

Maintain and update client files

Handle sales transaction reports for clients

⊙銷售助理

工作職責：

協助處理行政事務

維護、更新客戶檔案

爲客戶處理銷售業務報告

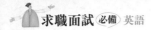

人·事·招·聘 ∘—∘ 程·式·設·計·師

⊙ **Program Designer**

Skills:

Familiar with computer

Expert at Office programs such as Word, Excel,

PowerPoint

Good at programming with C Language

Excellent in English speaking and writing

⊙ 程式設計師

專業技能：

熟悉電腦

精通 Word、Excel、PowerPoint 之類的 Office

程式

擅長 C 語言編程

英語說、寫很出色

人·事·招·聘 ·──· 電視編輯

⊙**TV Editor**

Position Requirements：

Minimum one-year experience in TV editing
is required. Knowledge of tape editing
preferred. Applicant must be bilingual and be
able to speak, read and write in both English
and Spanish.

Possible consideration will be given to college
degree (Mass Communications or related
field) with newsroom internship.

Brief Job Description：

Bilingual News Video Editor

⊙**電視編輯**

職位需求：

至少一年的電視編輯工作。瞭解錄影帶編輯
尤佳。應徵者必須為雙語言者，英文及西班
牙文說讀寫均擅長。大學學歷(大眾傳播系及
相關學歷)者，具新聞編輯室實習經驗者優先
考慮。

工作簡述：

雙語新聞編輯

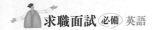

人-事-招-聘 ---- 軟體工程師

⊙ **Software/Programmer**

Company:IBM

Title:Software/Programmer

Posted:12/22/2016

Paying:30,000 to 35,000

Full/Part:FT

Working Location:Buffalo, NY (USA)

⊙ **軟體工程師**

公司：IBM

職稱：軟體工程師

刊登日期：12/22/2016

待遇：三萬至三萬五千元

專／兼職：專職

工作地點：美國紐約州水牛城

人事招聘 ⊙⊙ 出納員

⊙ **Cashier**

Required Skills:

Accounting Experience

Self-Motivated and Outgoing

Industrious

Willing to learn and grow

⊙ **出納員**

專業要求：

具會計經驗

個性主動、活潑

勤勉

願意學習及成長

人·事·招·聘 ···○··○ 企業聯合招聘 (一)

Position 1.2.3. requires minimum of 3 years supervisory experience.

1. 2. 3. 項的職位至少要有三年的主管經驗。

1. **Product/Training Officer**

College or above graduate

Familiar with retail operations

Fluency with English, willing to receive
extensive training

Capable of handling and developing training
programs independently

Previous experience in Product/Training

1. 生產／培訓部主管

大學以上學歷

熟知零售業運作

英文流暢，願接受額外的培訓

能夠獨立處理、發展培訓課程

有生產／培訓經驗

2. **Sales Operations Officer**

Male, above age 35

Experience in shop operations practice

Capable of establishing effective operation
routines in the shop level and store management

Initiative, independent, good communicator,
capable of leading a team

Willing to work under pressure and grow fast
with the company

2. 銷售業務主管

男性，35 歲以上

有商店管理的實際經驗

能夠在商店、倉管方面建立起有效的、作業
流程制度有創新

有進取心、獨立、善於溝通，並能領導團隊

能承受工作壓力挑戰，並能與公司一同快速
成長

3. **HR Officer**

College or above graduate major human
resources management

Familiar with recruiting/hiring/training practice
for both senior level personnel and entry level
staff

Familiar with retail operations

Good communicator, problem solver, and cheer
leader

3. **人力資源主管**

大專以上學歷，主修人力資源管理

熟悉資深及新進人員的招聘、雇用、培訓等事項

通曉零售業運作

善於與人溝通、解決問題並具備領導技巧者

4. **Art Director**

College or above graduate major in art related areas

Creative

Familiar with retail/shop operations

Capable of delivering ideas to present brand image and help shop display

4. **技術指導**

大學以上相關專業畢業

富有創造力

熟悉零售／商店業運作

能創新現有品牌形象，並協助店面展示

人·事·招·聘 ┄┄ 企業聯合招聘（二）

【Human Resource】

(Good English is required for all positions)

【人力資源部門】

（所有職務均要求英文流利）

1. HR Mgr./HR Sup.

2~3 years overall HR W/4~6 years mgt. Exp.

Master degree, banking background will be a plus

1. 人力資源經理／主管

2~3 年人力資源或 4~6 年管理經驗

碩士學位，有銀行背景者尤佳

2. Training Sup.

3+ years training courses design & development w/ trainer exp.

Master degree

2. 人力訓練主管

3 年以上培訓課程設計及發展培訓相關經驗

碩士學位

3. HR Specialist

4 years recruiting/staffing/adm. Exp.

3. 人力資源專員

4 年的招聘／任用／行政等相關經驗

人事招聘 企業聯合招聘（三）

BCQ Personnel Consultants

【**Administration**】

BCQ 人力資源諮詢公司

【行政部門】

1. Executive Secretary

5~8 years solid secretarial exp., in financial institute

Under age 32, good English and Japanese, B.A. degree

1. 執行秘書

5~8 年紮實的秘書經驗，有金融部門從業經歷

32 歲以下，英語及日語良好，學士學位

2. Secretary

2~3 years sec. or adm. Exp.

Good English, B.A. degree

Presentable

2. 秘書

2~3 年秘書或行政部門從業經驗

英文良好，學士學位

外表端莊

3. **Administrator**

1~3 years general affairs exp.

Well organized, able to set up office policy

3. **行政人員**

1~3 年一般行政管理經驗

組織能力良好，能建立辦公室規章制度

Part

4

履歷表及自傳

履歷表

　　履歷表是求職信中的主角，因為它是以列表形式出現，如果人事主管要處理數十或數百份的求職資料，較為省力的初步挑選就是先讀應徵者寄來的履歷表，所以履歷表的表現形式就顯得很重要。

在一份完整的履歷表中，須包括以下幾個重點：

一、個人基本資料

二、學歷背景

三、工作經驗

四、證明人

　　在履歷表中不須有完整句子，但必須將相關資料有系統的表達。求職信及履歷表須打字，除非對方特別要求書寫。此外，在履歷表上貼須上一張近期的照片。

自　傳

　　作為應徵使用的自傳，應當力求簡潔，以陳述事實為主，不求做細節的描寫，以便能在盡可能短的篇幅內，重點式地說明經歷。因此寫作內容是敘述性的文章，一般包括姓名、性別、年齡（或出生年月）、家庭情況、學歷、經歷等內容。

諺　語

If it were not for hope, the heart would break.

人靠希望而生。

【簡歷範例】基本資料

Name: Mary Chang

Birth Date: September 30,1990

Birth Place: Taipei, R.O.C

Sex: Female

Marital Status: Single

Weight: 52kg

Height: 157cm

Blood Type: AB

Asterism: Libra

Health: Excellent

Hobbies: Listening to the music, Literature, Yoga

姓名：張瑪莉

出生日期：1990 年 9 月 30 日

出生地點：中華民國台北

性別：女

婚姻狀況：未婚

體重：52 公斤

身高：157 公分

血型：AB 型

星座：天秤座

身體狀況：健康

興趣愛好：聽音樂、文學、瑜珈

【 Resume Sample 】 Personnel Supervisor

Christopher Nietopski

Tel: (02)8647-3663

Born: Nov. 18, 1977

Height: 180cm

Weight: 65kg

Birth Place: Buffalo, N.Y. USA

Marital Status: Single

Job Objective:

To apply experience and education to position in personnel administration in Sino-American Join venture.

Experience Pertinent to Objective:

From October 2008 to present Personnel Manager, BCQ Electric Appliance Group Company. Responsibilities include conducting salary surveys, establishing salary ranges and progression rates for each level, making job evaluation plans, questionnaires, application forms, etc., recruiting new employees, formulation and revising training programs, initiating an implementing programs to improve and utilize potential of staff members.

Education:

From September 2002 to July 2006, Majored in Personnel Administration at Ohio State University.

Special Skills:

Fluent both English and Chinese (reading/writing/speaking)

Experienced in operation of computer

References: Upon request

【履歷表範例】人事主管

克里斯多福・尼塔布斯金

電話：(02)8647-3663

出生：1977 年 11 月 18 日

身高：180 公分

體重：65 公斤

出生地：美國紐約州水牛城

婚姻狀況：未婚

工作目標：

在中美合資企業擔任人事管理的職務，能夠把自己的工作經驗及學歷運用到工作中去。

和工作目標相關的經歷：

自 2008 年 10 月至今擔任 BCQ 電器集團公司人事經理。工作責任包括：進行工資調查、確立工資等級及每級加升率、制定工作評估計劃、印製徵求意見表和申請表等，招聘新員工、提出並修改培訓計劃、制定並執行有關提高和利用職員工作能力的計劃。

學歷：

自 2002 年 9 月至 2006 年 7 月在俄亥俄州立大學主修人事管理。

特別技能：
中英語流利（讀／寫／說）
熟悉電腦操作操作
證明人： 需要即寄

實用例句

實用會話

人事廣告

履歷表及自傳

【 Resume Sample 】 Education

Maria Jones

Address:	No. 40, Lane 90, Sec. 2, Jhongshan Rd., Banciao Dist, New Taipei City. 220, Taiwan (R. O. C.)
Phone:	(02) 8467-3663
E-mail:	yadan@tpts5.seed.net.tw
Objective:	To obtain a position in financial analyst
Certificate:	CPA
Education:	B.S. in Economics to be obtained in June 2002

Related courses and scores on the 100 marking system:

Investment	86
Macroeconomics	90
Economic Decision-making	80
Accounting Principles	92
Money and Banking	84
Financial Management	92
Finance and Tax	92
Cost Accounting	85
Management Accounting	90
Economic Law	82

【履歷表範例】學歷資料

瑪莉亞・瓊斯

地址：中華民國台灣新北市板橋區中山路 2 段
　　　90 巷 40 號

電話：（02）8467-3663

電子郵件：yadan@tpts5.seed.net.tw

應聘職位：財務人員

證書：財務分析員

學歷：

　　　2002 年 6 月將取得經濟學學士學位
　　　相關課程及按百分制計算的成績如下：

投資學	86
宏觀經濟學	90
經濟決策	80
會計學原理	92
貨幣銀行學	92
財務管理	92
財務與稅收	92
成本會計	85
管理會計	90
經濟法	82

【 Resume Sample 】
Experience and Education

David Jackson

OBJECTIVE: Executive Secretary

Five years corporate administrative background

Expert at anticipating and solving complex problems

Effective communication at highest levels

Type 70 wpm

Know Word, Excel, Power Point, Network well.

EXPERIENCE:

(1) 1997 to present CNS Company Tokyo

    Executive Secretary to Marketing President

- Prepare daily, weekly and monthly reports, including sales plans, selling expense and sales per formance
- Draft correspondence, make travel arrangements, complete special projects as assigned
- Update and distribute store address list

(2) 1995 to 1997 BCQ Group Company Taipei

    Senior Secretary

- Supervised payroll, mail, and office supply
- Scheduled Training Program for 500+ employees
- Arranged agenda for managers' meetings

(3) 1994 to 1995 IBM Company New York

⊙ performed general office duties such as answering telephone calls, receiving visitors, arranging appointments, and drafting letters, and reports for director's signature.

EDUCATION:

1990 to 1994 Taiwan University

⊙ Graduated with honors

⊙ B.A., Secretary

INTERESTS:

Mountain climbing; Watching movie; Listening to the music

CONTACT:

Phone: (02) 8647-3663

Fax: (02) 8647-3660

E-mail: david@yahoo.com

REFERENCES1:

Chris Nietopski

Professor of Department of Economics Taiwan University

E-mail: chris@yahoo.com

Phone: (02)5687-2136

REFERENCES2:

Jack White
President of CNS Industrial Corporation
E-mail: jack@yahoo.com
Phone: (02)4567-1234

【履歷表範例】學經歷簡介

大衛・傑克森

應聘職位：執行秘書

具有五年的公司管理經驗

善於預測和解決複雜問題

具備高水平、高質量的商務溝通能力

打字速度為每分鐘 70 個字

熟悉 Word、Excel、PowerPoint 和網絡。

工作經歷：

(1) 1997 年至今，在東京 CNS 公司工作

　　任職營銷部總經理執行秘書

　　⊙編制日報表、週報表和月報表，內容包含
　　　銷售計劃、銷售成本和銷售情況

　　⊙起草信函，安排差旅，完成指定的任務

　　⊙更新並發布商店地址表

(2) 1995 年至 1997 年，在台北的 BCQ 集團公司
　　工作

　　任職高級秘書

　　⊙管理工資名單、郵件和辦公用品

　　⊙為 500 多名員工安排培訓

　　⊙安排經理會議日程

(3) 1994 年到 1995 年，在紐約 IBM 公司工作

　　任職秘書

⊙做些辦公室的一般工作，如：接聽電話，接待訪客，安排會議，起草信函、報告讓經理簽字

學歷：

1990 年至 1994 年，在台灣大學就學

⊙以優異的成績畢業

⊙取得秘書學學士學位

興趣愛好：

登山、看電影、聽音樂

連絡方式：

電話：（02）8647-3663

傳真：（02）8647-3660

電子郵件：david@yahoo.com

證明人 1：

克里斯・尼多福斯基

台灣大學經濟系教授

電子郵件信箱：chris@yahoo.com

電話:(02)5687-2136

證明人 2：

傑克・懷特

CNS 實業公司總裁

電子郵件信箱：jack@yahoo.com

電話：(02)4567-1234

【 Autobiography Sample 】

Dear Mr. Brown,

I am applying for the vacant position in your
Accounting Division announced your bulletin.

I have just passed the CPA exams and will receive a
Bachelor of Arts degree in accountancy from the
Taiwan University.

My courses in the accountancy curriculum have
given me not only the necessary theoretical
background but also extensive practical experience.
For each course I have worked many cases and
problems, including preparing systematic
accounting records and satisfactory statements for
hypothetical firms.

Courses in speech communication and business
writing have taught me how to communicate with
various business audiences. I can help your staff
present the immediate and reliable information
about costs and revenues the CNS needs to keep its
prices competitive and to increase its profits.

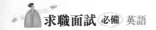

The enclosed resume summarizes my qualifications.
I would like to make an appointment for an
interview. I am looking forward to discussing with
you ways in which I can help CNS carry its tradition
of excellence further into the 21st century.

Sincerely,
Sophia Jones
Enclosure: Resume

【自傳範例】

親愛的布朗先生：

我從貴公司的簡報中獲悉了你們會計部空缺的職位，現致函應聘。

我剛好通過了註冊會計師考試，並即將取得台灣大學的會計學學士學位。

會計方面的課程使我不但掌握了必要的理論知識，而且獲得了廣泛的實踐經驗。我每門課都分析了不少的案例，解決了不少的問題，還為模擬企業做了系統的會計記錄，製作了令人滿意的會計報表。

語言交流和商務寫作課程使我獲得了怎樣和各種商務人士溝通的技巧。我能幫助貴公司員工，以提供及時可靠的財會訊息，以使 CNS 保持其價格優勢，增加利潤。

隨函附寄的簡歷概述了我的資格。我希望您能排個時間，對我進行面試。我非常盼望能和你們一道為 CNS 在 21 世紀的輝煌做出貢獻。

蘇菲雅・瓊斯敬上

附件：簡歷一份

【Autobiography Sample】

By Chris King

My name is Chris King. I was born on November 18, 1968, in Buffalo, N.Y. USA.

In 1992 I graduated from Cornell University where I majored in electronic engineering, and then I was assigned to work in an electronic apparatus factory as a technician for five years. During this period I gained some practical experience in designing and manufacturing several varieties of electronic apparatus.

In the fall of 1997, I was admitted to the Department of mathematics at Penn State University as a graduate student. Six months before I took the examination, I started to study higher algebra and analysis by myself in my leisure time. Since enrollment I have completed all the course required by the graduate program making straight A's both in my undergraduate and graduate courses. My performance in the graduate seminars of Differential

Calculus and Mathematical and Physical Formulas shows that I have got a good grasp of the fundamentals of mathematics.

I have been studying Chinese intensively for six months. I have attended a Chinese class taught by a Chinese teacher. And I have made great progress.

I have been trying to find any possible chances to expose myself to various kinds of experience. And I think that is what I'm going to do all my life.

【自傳範例】

克里斯·金撰寫

我叫克里斯·金，於 1968 年 11 月 18 日生於美國紐約水牛城。

1992 年畢業於康乃爾大舉，在那裡我主修電子工程。之後，我在一家電子器械廠當技師工作了 5 年。在此期間，我在設計、製造幾種不同類型的電子器械方面，獲得了一些實際經驗。

1997 年秋天，我考取賓州州立大學數學系研究生。在參加入學考試的前六個月，我利用業餘時間，開始自學高等代數和數理分析。自從入校以後，我已修完了所有的研究生必修課程，並且我的本科和研究生各門功課都全部獲得了 A 的好成績。我在關於微積分、數學、物理公式的研究生討論會上的表現，證明我已經完全掌握了數學基本原理。

我現在已進修中文六個月，我參加了一個由中國教師教學的加強班，且成績顯著。

我一直在尋找機會使自己能夠增長各種不同的經驗。今後，我仍將朝此方向努力。

【附錄一】職稱

1.工程技術類

Programmer	程式設計師
Computer Operator	電腦操作員
Systems Analyst	系統分析員
Systems Operator	系統操作員
Technician	技術員
Architect	建築師
Architectural Engineer	建築工程師
Art Designer	美術設計師
Chief Engineer	總工程師
Computer Engineer	電腦工程師
Consulting Engineer	顧問工程師
Engineer	工程師
Software Engineer	軟體工程師

2.商業會計類

Accountant	會計員
Auditor	查帳員
Bookkeeper	簿記員

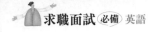

Export Clerk	出口人員
Export Sales Staff	外銷員
Financial Analyst	財務分析員
Market Analyst	市場分析員
Market Researcher	市場研究員
Marketing Representative	銷售代表
Merchandiser	商品業務員
Purchaser	採購員
Business Assistant	業務助理
Business Manager	業務經理
Export Sales Manager	外銷部經理
General Manager	總經理

3.行政管理類

President	董事長
General Manager	總經理
Human Resources Manager	人力資源部經理
Administrator	管理者
Supervisor	主管
Secretary	秘書

Project Staff	企畫人員
Personnel Manager	人事經理
Trainer	培訓專家
Production Manager	生產經理
Public Relations Manager	公共關係經理
Senior Consultant	高級顧問
QC Inspector	品質控制員

4. 文化教育類

President	大學校長
Professor	教授
Supervisor	督學
Lecturer/Instructor	講師
Researcher	研究員
Chief Editor	總編輯
Editor	編輯
Reporter	記者
Journalist	新聞記者
Columnist	報刊專欄作家
Interpreter	口譯員
Translator	翻譯員

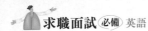

【附錄二】職業

房東	landlord
房東太太	landlady
房地產仲介公司	real estate agency
房地產仲介經紀人	real estate agent
房屋仲介	housing coordinator
傭人	servant
清潔工	house cleaner
清潔女工	cleaning maid
受僱者	employee
僱主	employer
退役軍人	ex-serviceman
前任總統	ex-president
已故總統	late president
陸海軍人	soldiers and sailors
官兵	officers and soldiers
當兵	go for a soldier
鉛管工	plumber
潛水員	aquanaut
男演員	actor

女演員	actress
歌手	singer
舞蹈舞家	dancer
音樂家	musician
魔術師	magician
鋼琴家	pianist
畫家、油漆工	painter
教師	teacher
教授	professor
中小學校長	headmaster
中小學女校長	headmistress
校長	head teacher
導演	director
編者	editor
作家	writer
記者	reporter
廣播員	announcer
雜誌記者	journalist
工人	worker
農夫	farmer

漁夫	fisherman
藥劑師	chemist
工程師	engineer
探險家	explorer
研究員	researcher
醫生、博士	doctor
內科醫生	physician
外科醫生	surgeon
藥劑師	druggist
牙科醫生	dentist
護士	nurse
水手	sailor
船員	seaman
飛行員、領航員	pilot
太空人	astronaut
駕駛員	driver
運動員	athlete
警察	policeman
警衛	security guard
偵探	detective

法官	judge
大陪審團	grand jury
律師	lawyer
律師	attorney
廚子	cook
廚師	chef
麵包師	baker
男侍者	waiter
女服務生	waitress
幫手(餐廳做端菜、收碗盤的人)	bus boy/girl
屠夫	butcher
店主	shopkeeper
書商	bookseller
裁縫師	tailor
軍人	soldier
郵差	postman=mailman
消防人員	fire fighter
圖書管理員	librarian
臨時看護嬰兒者	baby-sitter

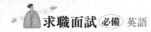

學徒	apprentice
工匠	artisan
工匠	craftsman
分析家	specialist
老闆	boss
製造商、製造廠	manufacturer
商人、(英)批發商、(美)零售商	
	merchant
小販、賣主	vendor
接待員	receptionist
電話接線生	operator
攝影師	photographer
劇作家	playwright
語言學家	linguist
植物學家	botanist
經濟學家	economist
化學家	chemist
科學家	scientist
哲學家	philosopher
政治家	politician

物理學家	physicist
考古學家	archaeologist
地質學家	geologist
火山學家	volcanist
數學家	mathematician
生物學家	biologist
動物學家	zoologist
統計學家	statistician
生理學家	physiologist
藝術家	artist
作曲家	composer
設計家	designer
雕刻家	sculptor
建築師	architect
服裝設計師	designer
模特兒	model
詩人	poet
空中小姐	stewardess
男性空服員	steward

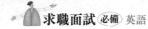
守門人、(搬運行李的)侍應生	
	porter
導遊	guide
監工	supervisor
辦事員	clerk
打字員	typist

求職面試必備英文

雅致風靡　典藏文化

親愛的顧客您好，感謝您購買這本書。即日起，填寫讀者回函卡寄回至本公司，我們每月將抽出一百名回函讀者，寄出精美禮物並享有生日當月購書優惠！想知道更多更即時的消息，歡迎加入 "永續圖書粉絲團" 您也可以選擇傳真、掃描或用本公司準備的免郵回函寄回，謝謝。

傳真電話：（02）8647-3660　　　電子信箱：yungjiuh@ms45.hinet.net

姓名：	性別：	□男　□女
出生日期：　年　月　日　電話：		
學歷：	職業：	
E-mail：		
地址：□□□		
從何處購買此書：	購買金額：　　　元	

購買本書動機：□封面 □書名 □排版 □內容 □作者 □偶然衝動

你對本書的意見：
內容：□滿意□尚可□待改進　編輯：□滿意□尚可□待改進
封面：□滿意□尚可□待改進　定價：□滿意□尚可□待改進

其他建議：

總經銷：永續圖書有限公司

永續圖書線上購物網
www.foreverbooks.com.tw

您可以使用以下方式將回函寄回。

您的回覆，是我們進步的最大動力，謝謝。

① 使用本公司準備的免郵回函寄回。

② 傳真電話：（02）8647-3660

③ 掃描圖檔寄到電子信箱：

　　yungjiuh@ms45.hinet.net

沿此線對折後寄回，謝謝。

2 2 1 0 3

 雅典文化事業有限公司　收

新北市汐止區大同路三段194號9樓之1

雅致風靡　典藏文化